**Walking t
Eleanor tr
speech, trie
to the que
inevitably ask, work out how she
could respond without telling
him about the baby.**

The baby.

Swiping her ID badge, she let her mind linger
on that thought. Now that she knew she was
going home, had decided on a future, she was
finally coming around to the idea that she was
actually going to have one.

And they'd be okay.

Eleanor knew that in her heart.

Carol Marinelli is a nurse who loves writing. Or is she a writer who loves nursing? The truth is, Carol's having trouble deciding at the moment, but writing definitely seems to be taking precedence! She's happily married to an eternally patient husband and mother to three fabulously boisterous children. Add a would-be tennis player, an eternal romantic and a devout daydreamer to that list, and that pretty much sums Carol up. Oh, she's also terrible at housework!

Carol now also writes for Modern Romance™!

Recent titles by the same author:

Medical Romance™

THE DOCTOR'S OUTBACK BABY
  (Tennengarrah Clinic)
THE BUSH DOCTOR'S CHALLENGE
  (Tennengarrah Clinic)
THE BABY EMERGENCY
  (Tennengarrah Clinic)
THE ELUSIVE CONSULTANT

Modern Romance™

THE ITALIAN'S MARRIAGE BARGAIN
THE BILLIONAIRE'S CONTRACT BRIDE

ONE NIGHT
IN EMERGENCY

BY
CAROL MARINELLI

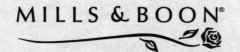

MILLS & BOON®

First published in Great Britain 2004
Harlequin Mills & Boon Limited,
Eton House, 18-24 Paradise Road, Richmond, Surrey TW9 1SR

© Carol Marinelli 2004

ISBN 0 263 83934 6

Set in Times Roman 10½ on 12 pt.
03-1104-45437

Printed and bound in Spain
by Litografia Rosés, S.A., Barcelona

CHAPTER ONE

'THERE'S been a bus crash!'

Eleanor's heart didn't sink as Mary Byrne placed her hand over the telephone receiver and mouthed the words to the rapidly gathering staff. Instead, it skipped into overdrive, galloping along way too fast.

Her mind was going at the same speed, too.

It was Saturday night and the emergency room was already full to bursting. Half the staff had rung in sick, courtesy of a flu bug that had started in Singapore and had somehow landed in Melbourne five days previously, so the place was being manned by only a couple of regular staff, along with rather too many agency nurses. And to cap it off, it was Eleanor's first night duty in the emergency department of Melbourne Central.

Actually, it was her first shift in Melbourne Central, full stop. She'd rather been hoping for a gentle easing into her new job, a slow introduction to a city emergency department after completing her training and graduation year in the country, but given that Mary Byrne was her mentor for the next three months it meant that for the most part they would be sharing the same shifts.

And as Mary had volunteered for a week of nights, by default, so too had Eleanor.

'A minibus crash,' Mary corrected, with a relieved sigh as she hung up the telephone and came over to address her staff. 'Which is a lot better than it first sounded, but that still means we've got twelve new patients arriving and at this stage we're not sure of the injuries. Ambulance Control is going to let me know more just as soon as they do.'

The red phone buzzed again and Mary answered it promptly, her stern face rigid with concentration and her thick Irish brogue direct and to the point.

'Lord help us all, then!' she exclaimed, slamming down the phone and coming back to her team.

'What is it?' Vicki, one of the few regular staff in the unit tonight, asked as Mary rolled her eyes and muttered loudly under her breath. 'Does it sound serious?'

'Oh, it's serious all right,' Mary retorted. 'The minibus that crashed happens to be filled with half the victors of some local rugby shield match. And, as luck would have it, the other half of the team was following behind, so no doubt they'll be descending on us too just to make things a touch livelier.'

'Where have you been, young man?' Mary asked as Pier, one of the agency nurses, joined the team. 'When the red phone goes off, you're supposed to come directly over.'

'*Oui*, I know, but I was putting cubicle six on a bedpan.'

'When the red phone buzzes, you ensure your patient's safety and then come to the nurses' station.' Mary fixed him with a stern glare. 'The only exception to that rule is if you're in Resus with a critical patient.'

'Are the injuries bad?' It was the first time Eleanor had spoken, her very newly registered nurse brain whirring ahead of itself, trying to imagine the types of injuries that would be arriving. For a full year she'd

been desperate to roll her sleeves up and tackle some
real emergency nursing, constantly frustrated by her
previous manager's attempts to thwart her, but now
that the moment appeared to have arrived, suddenly
Eleanor felt woefully unprepared.

'Cuts and bruises at this stage, one or two sound
as if they may have fractures, and the driver has a
nasty seat-belt injury—injuries I can deal with blind-
folded,' Mary thundered on. 'It's twenty-four young
men with too much C2H50H on board I can well do
without.'

'C2H...' Eleanor frowned, her voice trailing off as
she tried to, first, remember to look assertive and,
second, to work out just what on earth Mary was going on about now.

'You don't write that on their notes, mind,' Mary
said sharply as Eleanor dutifully wrote the mass of
letters and numbers down. 'They can smell like a
brewery, have slurred speech and be staggering as
they walk, but it would be very dangerous to make
any assumptions. The symptoms are the same as a
head injury and it won't go down too well in court if
it's even been hinted at in the patient notes. Have I
made myself clear?'

Eleanor nodded, but her frown remained.

'Now Resus is already full, so I'm going to head
in there and give Dr Heel a hand to clear the place.
Caitlin is on triage...'

'Helen, one of the agency nurses, has got an ICU
certificate,' Vicki ventured. 'Why don't you take her
into Resus with you? Heather and I can manage the
trolleys. And I'm sure Pier will be OK doing the cubicles.'

The look that Mary shot Pier told everyone present

that Mary was yet to be convinced. Pier might be divine to look at, might be incredibly eager to please, but the fact his English was heavily laced with a thick French accent was already causing more than a few problems.

'Sounds good.' Mary nodded. 'The rest of you will have to pitch in.' Her eyes again turned sharply to Eleanor.

'You did some Emergency in your grad year, didn't you?'

'I did,' Eleanor gulped, 'but it was a tiny country hospital, I wouldn't exactly call myself—'

'They have bandages in the country I presume?' Mary broke in, and Eleanor nodded nervously.

'Then you can have the walking wounded with Pier. Patch them up and move them on. And, for goodness' sake, once they're seen, do your best to get them into a taxi and as far from here as possible. I do not want my waiting room pumping with renditions of ''Swing Low Sweet Chariot'' or ''Danny Boy''.'

'We're in Australia, Mary,' Vicki pointed out with a grin. 'It's ''Waltzing Matilda'' here.'

'I don't need a song sheet,' Mary barked. 'Just get them treated and home to their mothers. Poor women!'

'Right.' She clapped her hands together. 'The first will be here in fifteen minutes or so which gives us time to do a quick clear up and get the place ready. Now, do we all know where we're supposed to be?'

Everyone nodded and started to drift off to their assigned tasks. Everyone except Eleanor. She didn't want to ask stupid questions, didn't want to take up Mary's valuable time, but given she'd been so specific about not writing in their notes, Eleanor had no choice but to ask exactly what it was she couldn't write.

'Mary, sorry to be a pain, it's just that I didn't understand what you meant when you said…' Eleanor swallowed hard, beating back a blush as the dispersing crowd all stopped, then turned to hear her question. 'What exactly is C2H…?' She glanced down at the scrap of paper in her hand where she'd hastily written the jumble of letters. 'C2H5OH?'

'Oh.' Mary gave her a very nice smile, which Eleanor was sure was false. 'I'm sorry, Eleanor, did I not explain myself clearly enough for you? I should have said that it's the chemical equation for ethanol.'

'Ethanol?' Eleanor repeated, the question in her voice evident, her bewildered eyes looking back up to Mary.

'It means drunk, Eleanor,' Mary said through strained lips. 'Does that make things clearer for you?'

'Much,' Eleanor replied, blushing to the roots of her hair.

'So take no nonsense from any of them,' Mary warned. 'A pretty thing like you will be like a sitting duck.'

'What's wrong?' Pier asked as they headed for the cubicles, noticing Eleanor's grimly set face. 'I also did not know that was the chemical equation for alcohol.'

'It's not that,' Eleanor retorted, shaking her head and marching on as Pier struggled to keep up.

'Then what ever is the matter with you all of a sudden?' Pier asked, clearly perplexed. 'The accident is not as serious as we first thought, we will all manage.'

'I know we will. It's not that, it's what Mary said about...' Eleanor shook her head angrily. 'It doesn't matter.' But the French clearly weren't fazed by a dash of emotion and Pier just followed her into the four-bedded treatment area, patiently waiting as Eleanor pulled a blanket around the shoulders of an elderly lady.

'What did she say that has you so angry? And you *are* angry, Eleanor,' Pier pointed out, watching as she stripped a case of a pillow, then rammed the unsuspecting foam rectangle into a fresh pillowcase.

'Well, so would you be.' Her eyes flashed as she spoke, two spots of colour burning on her cheeks. 'What on earth do my looks have to do with anything? Two hours into my first shift and the charge nurse is making little jabs about me being pretty.'

'But you are pretty,' Pier exclaimed. 'Beautiful even! Blond hair, blue eyes, a very feminine shape.' He made a rather lewd hourglass gesture with his hands, but somehow Pier could get away with it without causing offence. 'In fact, if I went for women, I would definitely go for you.' He watched as her lips tightened. 'I am not making things better, no?'

'No,' Eleanor replied, as they stripped the linen off a trolley and started to remake it in preparation for the new set of patients. 'Mary wasn't paying me a compliment, Pier, believe me. I've been up against a few "Marys" in my training and grad year and they all assume that a blond-haired, blue-eyed nurse can only be after one thing.'

'Sex?'

'A husband,' Eleanor wailed, thumping him none

too gently with the pillow. 'They all assume I'm merely biding my time until some suitable rich and good-looking man comes along.'

'We all are.' Pier grinned then, realising humour wasn't called for here, he stared at her thoughtfully for a long moment.

Eleanor wasn't just pretty, she was seriously beautiful. China-blue eyes heavily framed with dark lashes were an absolute contrast to the thick blond hair, which, unless she went to the hairdresser's weekly, was for once natural—all set off with a deep red rosebud mouth in a clear-skinned face and, given that Pier was rather more in tune with his feminine side than most men, he finally saw her problem.

'Eleanor, people can be jealous, say cruel things, make silly assumptions, pigeonhole you for how you look, how you talk, the job you do even. But you have to learn to let those hurtful comments go. Once you learn to be confident in who you are and what it is you want from life, those bitchy comments will just wash over you. Believe me, I know.'

Something in his voice reached Eleanor, something in Pier's stance told her that as happy and confident as he appeared life hadn't always been easy for him, and she gave a dejected nod. Pier's sympathetic advice and surprising understanding was all she needed to open up a touch.

'I didn't do too well in my grad year, that's why I finally made the decision to leave my home town and came here to get some experience.'

'You were in the country, *oui?*'

Eleanor nodded. 'The manager didn't like me—in fact, that's a massive understatement. Rita actively disliked me and in a tiny country hospital there aren't too many places to hide.'

'How small was it?'

'Three wards and a tiny emergency department, but when I say emergency it was more of a GP unit. Any real emergencies were transferred to the city.'

'So you do not have much experience in emergency nursing.'

'I would have had,' Eleanor said darkly, 'if only Rita had let me within a square mile of the place. Even though it was a tiny hospital, we covered a vast area. There were a lot of farming accidents, heart attacks, even a few suicide attempts. Of course, they were moved on to the city once they were stabilised, but until the paramedics arrived they were treated at the hospital. If Rita had only let me in a bit, I'd have had a lot of experience by now.' Eleanor gave a tight shrug. 'She treated me as if I'd barely got my first Guide badge, let alone a nursing degree. I spent my whole time in my so-called emergency rotation giving tetanus shots, putting on slings and bandages and making cups of tea for relatives. If I hadn't worked the wards for six months I'd have come out of my grad year none the wiser than when I'd started. I had to tell them at my interview, of course. They assumed I had some emergency experience, but when I told them how little I'd really done it was decided that I'd be rostered on with Mary for the next few months. If I last,' Eleanor added. 'She seems so fierce.'

'She needs to be, I guess. Imagine if this minibus crash had turned out to be really serious.'

'I suppose. And I know that I'm not much help at the moment, but I'm not completely useless. I might not be a great emergency nurse yet, but I have spent the last year working. It mightn't have been a busy teaching hospital, but we still had sick patients. I mightn't have learnt a lot in emergency but it was a different story on the wards. The country's crying out for nursing staff. Towards the end of my grad year I was even in charge of some shifts on the wards, yet Mary seems intent on treating me as if I'm a complete novice. At the interview she seemed so nice…'

'She is nice,' Pier broke in, smiling at Eleanor's dubious expression. 'Emergency nurses are a funny lot. ICU and coronary-care nurses are the same—cliquey, bitchy, always thinking that they're the busiest, most understaffed unit in the whole hospital.' As Eleanor's frown deepened, Pier's smile widened. 'But they're also the funniest, most down-to-earth, loyal lot you'll ever hope to meet, and once you're in you'll be there for life. You'll end up being Mary's biggest fan, I bet.'

'I doubt it,' Eleanor scoffed. 'And how come you're such a fan, when all she's done is roar at you?'

'She's testing me,' Pier responded easily. 'I guarantee if I make it through this shift, by the morning she'll be giving me the pick of the unfilled shifts on the roster. But I still don't understand,' Pier moaned, unfortunately getting back to the one subject Eleanor wanted to avoid. 'Why didn't this manager like you?'

'Well, in my written report Rita said that I wasn't assertive enough, that I was too busy focusing on petty details and not getting the job done.'

'What sort of details?'

Eleanor shrugged. 'Take Agnes over there.' She gestured to the elderly woman, who was sitting up now, her dirty feet sticking out from the blanket, her worldly goods wrapped in two carrier bags under the trolley.

'Can I have a bedpan, love? No hurry.'

'All night I give bedpans.' Pier rolled his eyes, ducking out and coming back two minutes later as they both helped the elderly woman on and waited outside the curtain. 'All night I tell you. You were saying?'

'My manager would have sent her off into the night, whereas I...'

'Would have let her sleep?' Pier ventured.

'And I'd have probably tried to arrange a social work referral for the morning, but Rita hated it. She said that I was slow, not good at finishing a job, that I left the place in a mess after I'd done a shift. But I didn't come into nursing just to check drugs and drips. I want to get to know my patients, to make a difference.'

Pier gave a knowing nod. 'It can be a bit like that sometimes. But what has all this got to do with you being pretty?'

Eleanor didn't want to go there, didn't really want to rake over old ground, but there was something about a night shift, something about sharing twelve hours with a virtual stranger you might never see again, and definitely something about Pier that made her open up. 'Apparently I hid behind it.' When Pier didn't respond she elaborated further. 'I'd bat my eyelashes to get my own way. Make a mess of things and then apologise, and apparently because I flashed a bit of cleavage all was forgiven.'

'You flashed your cleavage?' Pier's eyes were aghast.

'No.' Eleanor found she was smiling. 'It rather

tended to flash itself. We had to wear baggy old theatre gear and the neckline wasn't exactly tailored.
Well, I heard Rita saying that I used my…' Stumbling
over the word, she was infinitely grateful when Pier
chose a better one.

'Assets?'

'Thank you. I heard Rita implying that I used my
assets to gloss over the fact I was a lousy nurse.'

'She sounds horrible,' Pier stated loudly. 'Horrible
and ugly, too, I bet?'

'She was actually,' Eleanor admitted. 'But without
her on my side I wasn't going to get anywhere. I
really want to be an emergency nurse, Pier, it's all
I've ever wanted to be. That's why I decided to cut
my losses and move to the city.'

'So it didn't help when the charge nurse brought
up your ravishing looks the first night you were here?'
Pier asked perceptively, a smile twitching on his lips.
'Don't tell me, you want to be taken seriously—isn't
that what all the models say?'

'I'd settle for being thought of as a good nurse.'

'Then *be* a good nurse,' Pier said simply.

'Finished, love.'

They helped Agnes off, and then headed to the pan
room, the blue lights of the ambulance flashing past
the window as the first of the minibus accident ca-
sualties arrived. 'We'd better get out there.'

Eleanor gave a watery smile. 'Thanks, Pier, thanks
for listening.'

'Any time,' Pier said airily. 'If I can think of anything you can do to improve things, I will tell you on
our meal break. I am good at advice.'

'So am I.' Eleanor grinned as they headed across
the unit. 'So here's some—if you don't want to be

giving out bedpans all night, trying saying *yes* instead of *oui!*' She looked at his bemused expression. 'You're sending out subliminal messages, Pier. Every time one of the old ducks hears you say *wee,* they ask for a pan!'

'You really aren't just a pretty face after all!'

'No, Pier,' Eleanor turned her blue eyes on her new friend and fixed him with a determined glare. 'And I intend to prove it.'

As Mary had predicted, the arrival of the rugby team certainly livened the place up, not that it had been quiet before. But once the ambulances started arriving, in no time at all every cubicle, every trolley and every chair was packed to capacity, with staff rushing between them, prioritising patients, commencing treatments, pagers buzzing like unattended alarm clocks as the phones rang ever on. But somehow it was controlled chaos, a team stretched to its limits yet performing impeccably under Mary's fierce guidance, and for Eleanor, although busy, although more rushed than she'd ever been in her rather short nursing life, it was a night for falling head over heels in love with Emergency.

Real Emergency.

A team working independently at times, but always looking out for each other.

Monitors bleeping, blue lights flashing past, paramedics racing in, even Jim the porter providing invaluable back-up, wheeling patient after patient around to X-Ray, while quietly, in his own unobtrusive way, guiding the junior and new staff, taking Eleanor gently aside time and again and pointing out that Mary preferred portable drip stands to be secured to the trolleys, not IV poles pushed alongside them, that in an unexpected emergency it made transportation easier and that maybe she should give the nebuliser the doctor had just ordered before he wheeled the patient up to the ward.

His advice was invaluable and Eleanor took it with a grateful murmur of thanks, the clock whirring past midnight for the most part unnoticed, the waiting room gradually emptying as they worked their way diligently through the night.

'I'd like a hand in here, please, Eleanor!' Mary's flushed face appeared from the Resus doors. 'I need you to hold an arm for me.'

Which surely couldn't be as bad as it sounded!

Entering the hallowed area of Resus, Eleanor longed there and then for a day when this room was familiar to her, when she, like Mary, could glance at the wiggly lines on the monitor with a knowing eye and know, just know, that the patient hadn't gone into cardiac arrhythmia but instead the red dot attaching the electrode to the patient's chest must have fallen off.

'Mr Papadopoulos has had an inferior myocardial infarction. He's supposed to be going up to Coronary Care now, but he's not well enough to be moved.'

He certainly didn't look well enough! His eyes were closed as he struggled just to breathe, a grey, clammy face exhausted against the pillow, and Eleanor stepped forward nervously, unsure what she should do, but Mary didn't keep her in suspense for very long.

'I want you to shave his chest and reattach the dots,' Mary ordered, handing Eleanor the clippers.

'His drip has just packed in and I need to get IV access quickly.'

With shaking hands Eleanor did as asked, listening intently as Mary told her to rub the skin with alcohol swabs before applying the dots. 'They'll stick better,' she explained, turning her attention back to the useless IV bung she was trying to remove before inserting a new one.

'Heaven help us, do they teach these doctors nothing in medical school?' Pulling back the sticky plaster on the man's arm, she tutted away. 'Can you ever imagine putting sticky plaster on a man and not shaving him first? I'm sorry, Mr Papadopoulos, so very sorry, dear, but I really need to get this tape off.

'Now, Eleanor, hold his arm for me while I put another IV in and see how I shave the area before I put a wad of tape on. It might seem like a small detail but when Mr Papadopoulos is ready to have his IV removed, you can be sure he'll thank us for our foresight.'

'I'll remember.' Eleanor nodded. 'Is there anything else you need?'

'Could you ask Vicki to come and check some morphine for me?'

Which shouldn't have been a problem, but instantly Eleanor felt relegated. She was more than capable of checking controlled drugs, it was part of her job, but yet again Mary seemed intent on treating her like a student. 'I can check morphine, Mary,' Eleanor pointed out, quietly grinding her teeth as Mary effectively dismissed her.

'Just ask Vicki to come in, would you? You get on with emptying those cubicles. How is it going out there?'

'It's settling. Just a few more to be patched up and sent home.'

'Good lass.' Mary nodded. 'Save cubicle one for me, mind. I'll come and see him when I'm done in here. If you could just find Vicki for me and ask her to come in, that would be grand.'

'We're nearly there.' Pier gave a tired smile as Eleanor came out. 'I must have a drink or you'll be treating me for a faint. Vicki said to sort out our breaks between us—do you want to go first?'

'You go,' Eleanor offered, knowing Pier was just being polite. 'I'll just finish up here.'

'There's nothing to do.' Pier shrugged. 'Everything is under control. Mary said to leave cubicle one for her—he just needs some strapping and a tetanus injection, which I've already pulled up. Agnes is just sleeping it off in between asking for bedpans and the toddler in cubicle two just needs the doctor to listen to his chest now that his nebuliser is finished, then hopefully his parents can take him home.'

'Then go.' Eleanor grinned. 'Even I can manage that lot.'

It felt strange, being left alone in the department. Not that she was really alone, there were a few patients still around, a few doctors writing their notes up at the desk and the rest of the staff were bobbing in and out of various cubicles. But, standing at the nurses' station, Eleanor couldn't help but feel a bit smugly important, as well as nervous in case anything should come flying through the doors and she would, temporarily at least, be the one to deal with it.

'How much longer will he have to wait?' A ruddy-faced rugby player popped his head around the curtain and Eleanor made her way over, pulling out the casualty card from the clipboard.

'Shouldn't be long.' Eleanor peered at the card. 'He just needs some strapping and a tetanus shot.'

She expected an argument, after all she was just standing there, but instead the man disappeared behind the curtain and Eleanor listened with increasing impatience as the drunken guffaws got louder.

'How long will the doctor be?' The father of the toddler in cubicle two came over, a worried frown on his face, and Eleanor gave a sympathetic smile.

'Not too much longer. It has to be a registrar or consultant that discharges Marcus, and unfortunately they're both stuck in Resus at the moment. They know that you're waiting, though.'

'Fair enough.' He gave a tired shrug. 'He's just getting upset with all the noise, you know.' He nodded pointedly towards cubicle one.

'I do know,' Eleanor said grimly. She was about to tell him it shouldn't be much longer again, about to run with the usual spiel, but Pier's words had struck a chord.

Then be a good nurse.

Mary was just trying to share the workload by telling them to save cubicle one for her. Eleanor could just picture the scathing look if she came out of Resus and saw her standing at the nurses' station, twiddling her thumbs when there was still work to be done. Well, she'd learnt her lesson the hard way with Rita. By the time Mary came out, there wouldn't be a patient in the department *and* she'd have started cleaning the trolleys. Picking up the kidney dish with the tetanus shot in it, she smiled at Marcus's father. 'Leave it to me.'

Breezing into the cubicle, she shot her most withering stare at the five men standing around the trolley. 'Would you mind keeping the noise down, guys? We've got a young child next door and your noise is upsetting him.'

'*Sorry!*' The sarcastic response from the ruddy-faced man Eleanor could deal with, but when the other hangers-on started wolf-whistling Eleanor began to understand why Mary might have dealt with it better. But just as she started to wonder if perhaps she should leave the job to Mary after all, she found a rather surprising ally in her patient.

'Cut it out, guys.' His voice was deep and firm and brought an instant response, his five teammates instantly cutting the wisecracks and offering their apologies. For the first time Eleanor looked at her patient.

Then looked again!

For the past couple of hours she'd remained indifferent to the sight of six-foot-four, thick-necked, broken-nosed rugby players, but only a general anaesthetic could have rendered her indifferent to this one.

He was so huge that he made the gurney look like it belonged in the paediatric bay, yet there wasn't an ounce of fat on his solid frame that was way too big for the white hospital gown that stretched over his wide chest, blond tousled hair framed a rugged face and somehow he even managed to make the customary broken nose look endearing, but, then, one couldn't linger too long on his broken nose when navy eyes were attempting to focus. 'Sorry about this,' he said, gesturing to his raucous friends. 'They're getting bored.'

'Which would be understandable if they were two years old,' Eleanor replied crisply, determined not to let him see he was having the remotest effect on her. But her bossy nurse routine only delighted the crowd, the cat calls starting up again, growing ever louder, the whistles more piercing as Eleanor's blush darkened. But when little Marcus in the next cubicle started crying again, Eleanor's patience finally snapped. 'Right, you can all wait outside while I fix up…' She glanced at the casualty card. 'Mr Hunter.'

'Rory,' her patient offered, but Eleanor wasn't really listening. In best assertive nurse mode she shooed the last of the stragglers in the vague direction of the waiting room.

'I thought Mary was going to come and patch me up,' Rory ventured once they were alone.

'*Sister* Byrne is busy with a sick patient in Resus,' Eleanor answered crisply, 'so you'll have to make do with me.'

'That's fine,' he responded easily. 'And you are?'

'Sister Lewis.'

He was squinting at the name badge hanging around her neck, or at least Eleanor hoped that was what he was attempting to focus on.

'Do you have a first name?'

'Sister Lewis will do just fine,' Eleanor replied firmly. 'Now, you've already been stitched up.' Peering at the notes, she put them down before turning to her patient. 'It's the left thigh, isn't it?'

'I hope so, given that's the one they stitched.' Lifting his gown, he pulled back the dressing before, annoyingly—extremely annoyingly, in fact—reaching over to the silver trolley beside the gurney and helping himself to a wad of gauze.

'Please, don't.' Eleanor shook her head. 'The trolleys are sterile.'

'Really?' He gave her a slightly nonplussed look and Eleanor was forced to relent somewhat. 'Well, they're clean and I'm supposed to restock them soon. It doesn't make things easy when the patients help themselves.'

'Sorry.'

'It doesn't matter.' It didn't, but it was far easier to be bossy, far easier to be slightly cross, than focus on his thighs—very nice thighs, too, Eleanor thought reluctantly, extremely muscular, blond-haired thighs that needed to be strapped.

'I'll need to shave you.'

'Sorry?' There was no question that he was apologising this time and, clearing her suddenly dry throat, Eleanor forced a brisk smile.

'The doctor wants your thigh strapped,' Eleanor explained patiently. 'Because you're so, er, muscular he wants the sutures to have some support for a couple of days. That's why he wants you to have crutches as well…'

'But why do you want to shave me?'

'I don't want to,' Eleanor corrected. 'I *have* to. Believe me…' Echoing Mary's words, she flashed an efficient smile and said, 'You'll thank me for my foresight once the strapping comes off.'

'I'll look like a zebra,' Rory moaned. 'I read that hair grows back thicker and darker once you shave it.'

The grumbling smile he flashed at her wasn't making this any easier.

'Utter rubbish,' Eleanor scoffed, while feeling horribly guilty.

'It's true. I read it in a magazine—a women's magazine,' he added, as if it might make a scrap of difference.

'Well, if you'd read on, the magazine would undoubtedly have told you that the down side to waxing is sheer agony, which is what you'll get when the sticky plaster comes off if I don't shave you first. Wait there,' Eleanor added, fleeing for the safety of the stock cupboard and trying to even out her breathing as she located fresh heads for the clippers.

She could do this, Eleanor told herself firmly. Gorgeous men with massive hairy thighs were part and parcel of Emergency, so she'd better just buckle down and get used to coping with it.

'Right!' Pulling the curtain back, she marched in with the clippers.

'Right,' Rory responded glumly, as Eleanor swallowed hard and turned on the clippers, hoping his inebriated state would mean that he wouldn't notice her shaking hands.

'How much are you taking off?' Rory asked with a slight note of panic.

'Well, you need your thigh strapped,' Eleanor pointed out, 'not a small sticky plaster.' But despite her best efforts, the bossy nurse routine was getting harder and harder to keep. Despite his friends, Rory Hunter had been the perfect patient and Eleanor relented with an apologetic shrug. 'I'm really sorry about all this,' she mumbled. 'It really will grow back quickly.' She gave a wry smile. 'And itch like hell, too, no doubt.'

'Then I'm glad I'm not a woman.' Rory grinned. 'Must be hell, doing this every week.'

Eleanor laughed, really laughed. 'Well, generally we're not quite so hairy…' Her voice trailed off as his navy eyes attempted to meet hers, the room impossibly hot all of a sudden as the conversation tiptoed into dangerous territory.

'Roll over and I'll do the back,' Eleanor responded quickly.

He did as he was told. In fact, he was the model patient, lying quietly as Eleanor dressed the large cut and then strapped his thigh securely. 'Not too tight?' she checked, and he shook his head. He even lifted the sleeve of his gown without asking as she approached with his tetanus shot.

'Your arm might be a bit sore for a couple of days.'

'Thank you.'

'Right.' Happy with her work, Eleanor measured him for his crutches. 'Do you need a hand to get dressed?' she offered, praying he'd say no.

'I'll be fine.'

'And I'll need a deposit for the crutches,' Eleanor added, smiling up from the notes she was writing. 'Ten dollars.'

'I haven't got my wallet with me.' Rory patted his pockets. 'Maybe it fell out on the minibus.'

'Well, we need a deposit,' Eleanor said firmly, determined to retain a professional upper hand. 'It's a safety guard to ensure that people bring the equipment back that we loan. Perhaps one of your friends might be able to lend it to you.'

'It's OK, I've found it.' Balancing on one foot, he tried to pull his wallet out of his jeans and Eleanor made a mental note that next time she asked a disabled patient for the deposit it might be better to do it when they were lying down for, as it turned out, balancing on crutches and trying to locate his wallet in the back of his jeans wasn't the easiest feat.

Eleanor knew if she didn't intervene he'd be back in Theatre, having his scalp stitched.

'Let me help you.'

'I'll manage.'

'No, really.' Ducking behind him, she gave an almost imperceptible cough as she dipped her hand into his pocket and pulled out the offending article, handing it to him and feeling awful as he flipped it open, a single ten-dollar note the only cash he had on him.

'How much is in there?' Rory asked, squinting down.

'Ten dollars,' Eleanor gulped.

'Then take it.'

'How will you get home?'

'One of my friends will have some cash.' If she'd looked up she'd have seen a twitch of a smile on his lips. 'If not, I only live a couple of kilometres away. I'm sure I'll soon get used to the crutches.'

'Maybe you should just keep the money,' Eleanor offered. 'You can bring it in tomorrow or something.'

'Won't you get into trouble?'

'Probably,' Eleanor admitted, 'but I can't just let you hobble out of here with no means of getting home.'

'Taxis take credit cards now, Sister Lewis.' His face broke into a grin and Eleanor knew then he'd been teasing her. 'I'm sure I'll make it home in one piece.'

'Very funny,' Eleanor retorted. Gorgeous he might be, but Rory Hunter had just used up his last strike on Eleanor's sympathy card. 'Now, if you go out to Reception they'll happily call you and your friends a taxi.'

'I was actually hoping to catch up with—'

'Out that way,' Eleanor broke in, pointing to the exit sign. 'You might even be lucky and find a taxi out there already.'

'Well, thank you.' Carefully he moved one of his crutches to the other side and offered his hand. 'You were very, er, efficient.'

'All part of the service.' Her blush was coming back now. Seeing Rory Hunter dressed and standing and with his hand closing around hers, any hope of remembering he was a patient was fast fading. 'I'd better get on.' Gesturing to the exit once again, she turned back to her notes, only letting out a long-held breath when he finally hobbled out.

Right.

Surveying the mess her patient had created, Eleanor headed off to get a linen skip and returned to the cubicle just as Mary appeared, sweeping back the curtain with a bright smile.

'Finally, Rory!' Her smile faded as she eyed the mess. 'Where's Mr Hunter?'

'I strapped him up and sent him home.'

'He's gone?'

Eleanor nodded nervously. 'In a taxi. I moved him on quickly, just like you said.'

'And what's all the hair doing on the trolley?'

'I shaved him.' Mary's direct glare wasn't doing much for her confidence. 'As you said to do,' she croaked, 'so it didn't hurt when the strapping came off.'

'But this was a thigh injury,' Mary snarled. 'You put a piece of stocking over the thigh and then you strap it.'

'Oh.'

'What's this?' Picking up the ten-dollar note clipped

to the casualty card, she held it up, her accusing glare ever fiercer.

'The deposit for his crutches. I gave him a receipt and everything. He assured me that he'd bring them back.'

'Oh, I'm sure he will.' Mary sucked in her breath for a long moment before she carried on talking. 'In fact, I'd suggest you could even be seeing your crutches as early as tomorrow night.'

'Tomorrow night?' Again Eleanor had no idea what Mary was talking about. 'I thought they went to their GP for review and suture removal.'

'Well, that's the norm, of course,' Mary agreed with a small nod. 'But for staff we make exceptions.'

'Staff?'

'Some might call it a perk,' Mary rattled on, ignoring Eleanor's question. 'Not much of a perk, though. But we look after our own in Emergency. When staff or a member of their family is brought in to the department, it's an unspoken rule that the most senior staff look after them. You just broke that rule, Sister.'

'But I had no idea he was staff,' Eleanor said faintly. 'He never said.'

'Why did you think I asked you to leave him for me?'

Eleanor swallowed hard. 'To share the workload?'

'Do you not think I work hard enough?' Mary asked as Eleanor screwed her eyes closed, every word she uttered seeming to make this horrible situation worse. 'Did you think that by strapping a thigh and giving a tetanus shot, I'd somehow be showing that I was worth my salt?'

'Of course not.'

'You did remember to give him his tetanus shot, I presume?'

'Yes,' Eleanor whispered.

'Good!' Mary responded crisply. 'It would be a terrible thing if the consultant of the department came down with tetanus because one of his own staff forgot to give him his jab…'

'The consultant!'

'I'm back.' Pier breezed into the cubicle, refreshed from his break, his smile fading as he saw Eleanor's paling face. 'Sorry, am I disturbing something?'

'Not at all, Pier,' Mary responded. 'In fact, we were just finishing.'

'Mr Hunter has already gone?' Pier asked, a curious smile on his face as he eyed the trolley littered with dark blond hairs.

'Minus ten dollars and some body hair,' Mary said. 'Sister Lewis here took it upon herself to treat him. Not only treat him—she practically threw him out of the department into a waiting taxi.'

'I don't understand…' Pier's voice trailed off and Eleanor waited, waited for an explosion, for that Irish temper to ignite, but, as she was about to find out, not only didn't she know the first thing about Emergency nursing, she didn't know the first thing about emergency nurses' sense of humour. Instead, she watched in stunned confusion as Mary Byrne threw her head back and laughed, followed a moment later by Pier.

And they didn't just laugh, they roared.

Roared till the tears were falling down their cheeks. And every time Eleanor thought it was over, thought her torture might have ended, they'd catch sight of the trolley and start to roar again.

'It's not funny, you two,' Eleanor finally snapped, protocol thrown to the wind, close to tears now and wishing the night would just end.

'Oh, but it is, my dear,' Mary sobbed, wiping her eyes with one hand as she held her aching side with the other. 'We'll feast on this for weeks!'

CHAPTER TWO

SO MUCH for patient confidentiality.

Rory Hunter's injuries and treatment became seemingly the sole topic of conversation for the entire hospital.

At least it felt that way for Eleanor as she stumbled through her week on nights. Every ward she took a patient to, she was sure the nurses were nudging each other. Even the cleaners seemed to be smiling as they quietly mopped the long lonely night corridors as Eleanor made her way back. But as hard as the nights were, nothing was going to compare to facing the man himself and it took a good deal of foundation and a lot of deep breaths to arrive at the nurses' station for handover the following Monday.

'You'll be working the trolleys,' Mary instructed. 'Anything you don't understand, you ask me, not the nurse who happens to be passing, not the doctor who looks approachable. You ask me. Until you feel confident to make decisions for yourself, I'm the one you run things by.'

'Fine.' Eleanor nodded, her hackles immediately rising. She was tired of Mary constantly talking down to her and treating her like a child that needed to be told everything not just twice but very loudly, too.

'Good. Now, in cubicle eight is an Emily Nugent. She's ninety-four with end-stage COAD. What does that stand for?'

'Chronic obstructive airways disease,' Eleanor answered with a slight edge to her voice. She may not be the most experienced of nurses but she wasn't a complete hick and it was time Mary stopped treating her like one. Taking a deep breath first, Eleanor looked the older woman straight in the eye. 'I'm not a student, Mary, I'm not even a grad nurse. I'm a registered nurse and I did do some nursing before I came to Melbourne Central. We do have COAD patients in the country.'

'Do you, now?'

'Yes,' Eleanor replied curtly.

'Well, as I said, Miss Nugent is end stage. Now, she's been seen by the medical registrar and she's not for any active treatment and definitely not for any heroics. You'll not be offended if I ask you to confirm you know what that means.'

'She's not to be resuscitated,' Eleanor responded, ignoring Mary's sarcasm and still trying to look her in the eye but it was getting increasingly hard.

'Correct. Now, that might seem like a very basic question, but the fact is, unlike the wards, all patients who come through our doors are resuscitated unless it's documented otherwise, and the last thing poor Miss Nugent needs is a bunch of over-zealous doctors jumping on her ninety-four-year-old chest. Now, we're to make her comfortable while the bed manager tries to find a bed for her on the wards.'

'Does she have family with her?' Eleanor asked as they headed for cubicle eight.

'She has no one, so our job…' Mary paused outside the curtain, opened her mouth as if to speak then instead gave a small nod. 'In we go.'

Eleanor's jury was still out on her feelings for Mary Byrne the woman, but if ever Eleanor made it into an emergency room at the grand old age of ninety-four she hoped there would be an equivalent of Mary Byrne there to look after her. For though Eleanor had looked after a few terminal patients, though she had worked alongside a lot of nurses, no one held a candle to the way Mary gently fussed over the frail elderly woman, chatting softly to Emily as if they were old friends as they turned her onto her other side to relieve the pressure from her emaciated hips, gently stroking her forehead as the old lady whimpered in pain.

'It's OK, Miss Nugent,' Eleanor said softly. 'I know it's uncomfortable while we move you, but you'll feel a lot more comfortable once we've settled you.'

A tiny nod indicated a response and as a frail thin hand peeped out from under the sheet, Eleanor took it and gave it a gentle squeeze.

'Do you have any pain, Miss Nugent?'

Another nod was punctuated by a grimace. 'Em.'

'You like to be called Em?' Eleanor checked, stroking the frail skin beneath her fingers. 'Then that's what we'll call you. My name's Eleanor.'

'Give her hair a brush,' Mary instructed, rummaging through Emily's bag and pulling out a brush. 'While I go and find someone to check...' She paused for a moment, taking the brush herself and running it through the straggly hair. 'Miss Nugent, I mean Em,' she said softly into the elderly women's ear, 'Sister and I are just going to get you some medicine that will make you more comfortable.'

Eleanor almost had to run to keep up with Mary's brisk strides, but she was walking on air, thrilled that far from the dressing down she had expected Mary finally seemed to be coming around.

'OK, you need to use your swipe card to gain access,' Mary instructed needlessly. Eleanor had checked plenty of drugs in her week in Emergency, just not the controlled ones, but Mary, it would seem, couldn't pass up any chance for a quick lecture. 'And it pays to look over your shoulder before you go in— there can be a few undesirables hanging around just waiting to get in here.' A loud tut came out of her pursed lips as they pushed open the door and stepped inside. 'For the love of God! Would you believe that her medical registrar has written in his notes that he wants her to have morphine, yet he hasn't written up an order?'

'Do you want me to page him,' Eleanor offered, but Mary shook her head.

'He'll be starting his ward round now, it will be ages till he comes back down.' She shook her head again. 'I'll have to ask one of our doctors to do it, which isn't really fair on them, given Miss Nugent's status. They'll need to examine her and go through all the notes, which will take for ever. Oh, poor Miss Nugent.' As she pulled open the drug-room door Eleanor went to follow, but instead ducked back in as Mary's tone took on a distinctly friendlier note. 'Rory! The very man who can help.'

'What's the problem?'

Eleanor heard him before she saw him, cringing behind the door as Mary patiently explained the problem. 'The med reg will be doing his rounds and the poor lady's in distress. I don't want her to be prodded and poked just for the sake of it.'

Eleanor had rather hoped her next glimpse of him

would have been from a safe distance, that somehow she could have blushed unnoticed from afar, but instead six feet four of dark-suited, heavily aftershaved, damp-haired, masculine beauty squeezed himself into the drug room and gave her the briefest of nods.

'Good morning, Sister.'

'Morning,' Eleanor croaked.

'Could I see the notes, please?'

Her hand was shaking so much as she passed them to him, she was practically fanning him, but Rory didn't seem to notice, taking them with a murmur of thanks and then reading them through carefully. If he'd looked gorgeous in jeans and a T-shirt, he looked divine in a suit, those sexy dark blond curls combed back smoothly now, and first impressions clearly counted for nothing because Rory Hunter up close and personal looked every inch the consultant. He had an authoritative air, a distinguished look about him, nothing like the tousled man who had lain on the gurney just over a week previously.

But it wasn't just his hunk status that was causing a tremor to ripple through Eleanor. As senior as Mary and Rory were, Eleanor wasn't quite sure how she'd react if Rory just wrote up the morphine without laying eyes on the patient. It was all very well for Mary to call in a favour, all very well for Rory to trust in her, but as junior as she was it was still Eleanor's responsibility, if she were to sign her name in the drug book, to assure that due care had been given.

'I'll need to see her,' he said finally, and Eleanor let out a relieved sigh. 'I'll do my best not to upset her, though. Can one of you give me a hand?'

'Eleanor will go with you.' Mary beamed. 'And

thank you for this, Rory, I know it's not your problem.'

'If it's in my department it's my problem.' Rory shrugged, nodding to Eleanor to follow him.

It was the longest walk of Eleanor's life. Apologies bobbed on her tongue, but she bit them back. Clearly Rory wanted to pretend the whole embarrassing incident hadn't happened, which suited her just fine.

'It won't take long.' Rory gave a brief on-off smile as they reached the cubicle and, utterly unable to look at him, Eleanor gave a small nod. 'Is everything all right, Sister?'

'Fine,' Eleanor croaked.

'You do understand why I need to examine her?'

She did but, given a sudden dry throat and a face a darker shade of purple, even a simple 'yes' was impossible at the moment and a rather unconvincing nod was the only response she could manage, putting her hand up to pull the curtain back, wanting to just get inside. But Rory had other ideas, calling her back and addressing her sharply.

'While morphine will certainly make Miss Nugent more comfortable, it will also compromise her level of consciousness and her breathing.' Rory's eyes were boring into her as Eleanor stared down at her hands. 'Now, I know it's not ideal that I have to examine her again, and I know it must be rather annoying for you to have to walk all the way from the drug cupboard and then back again, but for the record, Sister, I'm not prepared to write up a strong injection like morphine without having first seen the patient.'

'Mr Hunter.' Somehow she found her voice, somehow she managed to tear her eyes from her hands and look up at him, if not into his eyes at least in general direction of his face. Uncomfortable she may be, facing him, but Rory Hunter's biting sarcasm needed to be addressed. They mightn't have got off to the best start the week before last, she might have come across as the worst nurse in the living memory, but his hint at laziness was unjust and unfair. 'I have no problem with you examining Miss Nugent. In fact, I was thinking back in the drug room that had you just written up morphine for Mary, I would have refused to give it. I most certainly wouldn't be happy giving a strong drug to a patient as sick as this one, prescribed by a doctor who hadn't even laid eyes on her.'

'Good,' Rory replied crisply.

'And the inference that I somehow resent making two trips to the drug room is unfair.'

'Then I apologise.'

'Oh.' Eleanor blinked at him.

'You seemed a bit uptight. I assumed that was the reason.'

'Well, it wasn't.'

'Clearly.' He cleared his throat. 'Now, let's have a look at the patient.'

Any grievances were left firmly at the cubicle's entrance. Rory Hunter's bedside manner was impeccable. Politely he introduced himself to Em, his huge hands gently closing around her frail wrist as he located the flickering pulse, before pulling his stethoscope out of his pocket, even rubbing the bulb to warm it before listening to her chest.

'Can you help me sit her forward so I can listen to her back?'

They gently lifted Em forward, Eleanor talking soothingly as the old lady whimpered at the intrusion.

'Nearly done,' Rory soothed as they laid her back

against the pillow. 'We'll go and get you that medicine now. You'll soon be much more comfortable.

'Poor thing,' he added as they got outside. 'How long till she gets up to a ward?'

'I'm not sure. Mary said that the bed manager is trying to locate a bed, but the medical and geriatric wards are all supposedly full. Perhaps a few will be freed up after the ward rounds.'

'Hopefully she'll make it till then,' Rory said pointedly, scanning the department with those navy eyes. 'It looks like Mary's tied up. I'll go and get the keys off her and check the drug with you—the patient's already waited long enough.'

Which was the last thing she needed, but at least it meant Em would soon be more comfortable, Eleanor consoled herself as again she found herself in the drug room with him.

'We'll just give her 2.5 mg for now,' Rory said, talking aloud as he wrote up his notes. 'If that doesn't settle her, let me know, but she's so tiny I'm sure it will be plenty.'

'Sure.'

Of course, because Mary had never let her so much as touch the sacred controlled drug keys, it seemed to take for ever to work out which one to use, especially with Rory tapping his pen impatiently as she fumbled. 'Sorry.' Pulling out the drugs, she showed him the morphine vials. 'Twenty ampoules, after this one nineteen.'

'Agreed.'

Thankfully he took it from her to pull it up, so at least Eleanor was spared the indignity of getting a thin needle into tiny ampoule with a hand that wouldn't stop shaking.

As Rory pulled up the drug, Eleanor filled in the drug book, carefully writing in the patient details and the amount of morphine to be both given and wasted before signing her name.

'All done?' he checked.

'I just need your signature.'

'Sure.' She waited as he signed, stood with keys poised, ready to close the cupboard once he'd finished with the drug book, but Rory seemed to be taking an inordinate amount of time to sign his name.

'Is everything all right?' Eleanor asked anxiously.

'Fine.' With a flurry he signed his name then waited patiently while she locked up. 'Sister Lewis.' His lips twitched around the words and Eleanor stood frozen as he continued with a grin, 'So *that's* the reason you were so uptight.'

'Obviously,' Eleanor muttered through gritted teeth, the drug room seeming to implode on them as Rory started to laugh.

'It was you who...'

'Shaved you? Yes! Charged you ten dollars for crutches? Yes!' Eleanor answered hotly. 'I can't believe you've only just recognised me.'

'I recognised your name,' Rory corrected, still laughing as her blush deepened. 'Sister Lewis. And before you assume I was blind drunk last week, I wasn't.'

'I beg to differ,' Eleanor scoffed. 'You could barely focus! You didn't even recognise me this morning!'

'Oh, I'm sure I'd have remembered *that* face.' Rory grinned. 'But the simple fact of the matter is I lost my contact lenses in the accident. And if you don't believe me, wait till you work a Saturday night with me and half the department's scrabbling around the floor because I've lost a lens. I really can't see beyond my nose without them.'

'You'd lost your contact lenses?'

'I'm as blind as a bat without them,' Rory explained, his smile fading as he registered the tense look on her face. 'Are you all right, Eleanor?'

'Shouldn't I be asking you that?' Eleanor bristled. 'Given that you were the patient I mistreated.'

'You didn't mistreat me,' Rory said slowly, a frown marring his forehead as he eyed her thoughtfully. 'You were very—'

'Efficient,' Eleanor finished for him. 'You already said.'

'Hey, Eleanor, you really are upset, aren't you?'

'Oh, what do you care?' Eleanor snapped, then, remembering Rory was a consultant and she a very new nurse, she gave her head a small shake, running a worried hand across her forehead before dragging her eyes up to his. 'I'm sorry. Sorry for snapping just now and I'm sorry about the other night.'

'Forget it.' Rory shrugged. 'Look, I never meant to upset you.'

'Then why did you…?' Tears were brimming now, angry, hurt tears, a whole week of humiliation rearing to the surface now. 'Why didn't you tell me you were the consultant of the department? Why on earth did you let me make such a fool of myself?'

He never got a chance to answer, the door opening and Mary bustling in. 'There you both are.' Taking the kidney dish with the drug in it, she gave Eleanor a wink. 'You took so long I thought you must be shaving the other thigh.'

'Mary.' Rory's voice was stern. 'That's enough

about that. Eleanor's upset enough, without having everyone constantly going on about it.'

'Well, you should have thought of that,' Mary scolded with another wink, flying out the door, 'before you let some pretty young blonde thing shave your leg.'

Left alone Eleanor gave a brittle smile, as Rory stood there grim-faced.

'Well, I guess Mary just answered my question.'

Without waiting for his response, she turned on her heel, pulling hard on the metal handle and escaping into the corridor, her mind pounding as she raced to catch Mary.

She'd been a fool to think a new start would change things. It was her old job all over again!

Worse even.

Slowing down, she caught her breath for a second, and reluctantly acknowledged why.

He'd seemed so nice.

Oh, not the Rory Hunter who'd paraded in this morning, but the tousled-haired rugby player she'd met that Saturday night. The man who'd made her laugh, the man who'd gently teased her. A man who, despite her embarrassment, despite her scorching shame around their first encounter, she'd been secretly looking forward to seeing again.

Secretly pleased she'd be working alongside.

Well, not now, Eleanor thought darkly, picking up her pace and heading for the cubicle. Rory Hunter was as bad as the rest and Mary was just the same.

She'd been a fool to think things would be different here.

The morning passed in a horrible blur. For once, Mary's razor-sharp tongue seemed to have softened and for the most part she left Eleanor alone with her blushes as she gritted her teeth and tried to ignore the sniggers from the rest of the staff every time Rory came within a square mile of her.

'Mary said you were to go to lunch now.' Vicki smiled as she came over. 'I'll watch your patients while you're gone. What's happening?'

'Not much,' Eleanor sighed. 'Most are waiting for beds.' She took Vicki around the cubicles, giving her a brief handover of all the patients in her care, but as they got to cubicle eight Eleanor stepped inside, frowning as she felt Em's pulse. 'Her pulse is very irregular.'

'Her respiration rate's down, too,' Vicki observed, glancing at the casualty card. 'She looks very comfortable, though,' she added as they stepped outside. 'I don't think Mrs Nugent will be going to a ward.'

'It's Miss Nugent,' Eleanor corrected, 'but she likes to be called Em.'

Vicki nodded, writing the preference in red on the card and circling it—something Eleanor hadn't thought to do. 'Go on, you'd better go.'

Eleanor nodded but her heart wasn't in it, her eyes dragging back to cubicle eight. 'I might just sit with Em for a while,' she said as Vicki's eyes widened. 'I can have my lunch in there.'

'Are you mad?' Vicki shook her head. 'Mary would have a fit. No, go and have a proper break. I'll keep an eye on her.'

And she would, Eleanor knew that. In a little while Vicki would pop her head in, pat the old lady's hands and check that she was comfortable, but that would be it. And no one was being cruel, no one was neglecting the patient or being indifferent. There simply wasn't time for one-on-one nursing when it wasn't intensive, weren't enough nursing hours allocated in Emergency to hold an old lady's hand for an hour or two.

But that was what nursing was about for Eleanor.

That was the nurse she wanted to be, the nurse she'd sworn she would be, and she wasn't going to changer her priorities now.

Of course, Mary had to be talking to Rory, but Eleanor was tired of hiding from him anyway, tired of blushing at each and every turn.

'Can I have a word, Mary?'

She glanced down at her watch. 'I thought you were at lunch?'

'I am.' Eleanor gave a small shrug. 'I was wondering if I could take it in cubicle eight.'

'Cubicle eight?' Mary stared at her, nonplussed. 'But Miss Nugent's in there.'

'I know, I just…' Eleanor faltered, aware Rory was staring at her, too. 'She's near the end now and she's on her own…'

'Vicki will watch her,' Mary said dismissively. 'Now, for the last time, will you go to lunch?' Turning her attention back to Rory, Mary resumed her conversation but Eleanor most definitely hadn't finished.

'I am going to lunch, Sister Byrne.' Eleanor cleared her throat. 'And if you need to find me for anything, I'll be in cubicle eight.'

CHAPTER THREE

'HEY, Em.'

Pulling a chair over beside the gurney, Eleanor peeled the wrap off her Vegemite sandwiches before settling back in her seat and taking the old lady's hand with one hand while holding her lunch with the other.

As Vicki had said, Em seemed comfortable, her breathing shallow, her weatherbeaten, heavily lined face relaxed now, her hand slack as Eleanor held it. But whether or not Miss Nugent knew that someone was there, Eleanor wanted to stay.

Didn't want ninety-four years of life to go out un-acknowledged.

And probably the last thing this tired old lady needed was the neurotic chatter of a tense twenty-three-year-old, didn't need to hear about the dramas going on in the nurse's life as she slipped out of this world. So Eleanor kept quiet, apart from the occasional word of support, a gentle reminder that some-one was near, that someone thought that Miss Emily Nugent was a very important lady indeed.

Who knows? Eleanor thought as Em's breathing gradually slowed down. Seventy-one years from now, she herself would look back on her life and today wouldn't even merit a thought, today would be so insignificant in her life span it wouldn't even rate a mention.

It would.

How could she ever forget the loneliness that

gripped her now as she held onto Em's hand? The horror of living in a very tiny bedsit in a very big city and surviving on Vegemite sandwiches till her very new bank account finally had some funds paid in. Or the awful quiet nausea of leaving her family behind, parents, brothers, sisters, friends who in turn had told her she was crazy to leave, all insisting she was over-reacting. That things would get better soon.

Maybe they would have, Eleanor mused as she sat there quietly. Maybe in time she'd have learned to stand up to Rita, but her problems with her old manager hadn't been the only reason Eleanor had left.

How could she tell her family and friends that somehow the country wasn't quite enough for her any more? That she yearned for the nursing experience only a city hospital could give?

Needed to find out if she could actually do it.

Could be the emergency nurse she truly wanted to be.

And what had she done?

Her first shift in, she'd made a complete and utter fool of herself, acted just like the bimbo Rita had hinted she was, but worse, far worse than that, Mary's throw-away comment that Rory hadn't been able to rebuff.

How could she work alongside him now?

How could she command and give respect to a man who had treated her like that?

'Sister Lewis, I was wondering if I could have a word.'

How long he'd been standing there Eleanor had no idea. Normally she would have stood as a consultant entered, but, given she was on her lunch-break, given she was holding Em's hand and given the fact she, quite frankly, couldn't be bothered, Eleanor instead just turned her head a fraction.

'I'm a bit busy at the moment,' Eleanor responded with absolutely no rudeness intended. Emily Nugent might not be at the top of the emergency department's priorities but for a little while at least she was at the top of Eleanor's.

'I can see that.' Rory came over, casting a knowing eye over the patient, before turning his gaze to her. 'However, I was rather hoping we could talk.'

'My lunch-break ends in fifteen minutes. I could come to your office then.' Her voice was flat, her attention turned back to Em, but as Rory coughed uncomfortably she felt a blush suffuse her cheeks as he started to speak again.

'I was hoping to keep this off the record.'

'Sorry?' Finally she looked at him, taking some solace in the fact that he looked as uncomfortable as her.

'Perhaps I could see you after work, in the canteen maybe. I'd really rather make this an unofficial chat, though of course if you'd rather it was all documented…'

'Documented?' An incredulous note entered her voice and Eleanor fought quickly to control it, determined not to cause Em any discomfort. Squeezing the old lady's hand gently, she stood up, 'I'll be back in a moment, Em,' Eleanor whispered, before following Rory to the other side of the curtain.

'May I ask what all this is about?' Her five-foot-two frame, even extended to its full indignant height was no match for Rory, but it didn't stop her from trying. 'I happen to be on my lunch-break, sitting with a patient, and you have the audacity to storm in—'

'I didn't storm in,' Rory interrupted, but Eleanor was in full swing now.

'You have the audacity to *walk* in then, and invite me to an off-the-record little chat. Can I ask what I'm supposed to have done wrong now?'

'Nothing.'

'It doesn't sound like nothing,' Eleanor retorted. 'In fact, it sounds as if I've killed someone. So, please, Mr Hunter, don't keep me in suspense. What on earth have I done wrong now?'

'You've done nothing wrong.' His voice was insistent, stern even, enough to stop her tirade. 'In fact, from where I stand, you would appear to be the wronged party.' He took a deep breath. 'I had a word with Mary.'

'Oh.'

'About her little comment.'

'Oh.'

'Now, Mary meant nothing by it, it's just her sense of humour. But, as I pointed out to her, it could quite easily be taken the wrong way. And before you say "oh" again,' Rory carried on quickly as Eleanor's mouth opened, 'if you'd rather not speak off the record then that's entirely your prerogative. I can have a word with Personnel and arrange a mediator—'

'Mr Hunter.' Eleanor's voice was firm, assured even, but her face was flushed and her eyes glittering as she spoke. 'I made a mistake that Saturday night, a stupid, naïve mistake that I'd dearly love to get over. But now not only am I the laughing stock of the entire hospital but, instead of being afforded the dignity of dying quietly, of hoping this whole blessed thing will just blow over, I'm now being pigeonholed as some raving militant and we're now talking me-

diation.' When he didn't answer Eleanor carried on,
her fury, her scorching shame laced in every last
word. 'Being the talk of the hospital I can take,
heaven knows I've been there. Being thought of as
an idiot, yep, been there, done that, too. But if you
think I'm going to sit with some mediator and go over
the trivial events of that Saturday night just to save
you and Mary from a harassment claim then you've
got another think coming.'

'Was that a yes or a no?'

So bland was his tone in comparison to hers,
Eleanor realised she might have overdone it, pulling
her defiant eyes away and settling for the polished
tiles as she struggled to remember the point she'd
been so passionately arguing. 'What was the question?'

Had she looked up she would have seen Rory's lips
twitch, but from her bird's-eye view of the floor she
had to make do with his rather deep, very official
voice. 'On or off the record? On the record means
my office at three, off the record means a coffee in
the canteen around five.'

'I finish at four,' Eleanor responded, scuffing the
floor with her foot and wishing it would simply open
up and swallow her. 'But I have to go to the pay
office, so I guess I could hang around.'

'It would be much appreciated.'

'Anything else?'

'Nothing that won't keep till five.' As she turned
to go he called her back. 'Eleanor, Mary wasn't being
dismissive when she told you to go to lunch. Who
knows what's going to come through the doors this
afternoon? You need to use your breaks properly,
have something to eat, get away for a while…'

'Do you?'

He smiled at her perception.

'Not enough, I guess. But it is important to switch off sometimes.'

'I wouldn't have switched off, though. I'd have spent the whole time thinking about Em.' She gave a small shrug. 'Please, don't make this a big deal, Mr Hunter. I've had a break, I've had something to eat and, for what it's worth, I feel as if I've actually done some nursing today.'

Had she made a difference?

Oh, she hoped so.

As kind as Vicki was, as professional and courteous as she might be, never did Eleanor want to fill out the paperwork that heralded the end of a life with a hasty pen and a brisk manner, never did she want to become so blasé about the lives she was privileged to share that she could walk away without shedding a tear when, however old, however ready, they ended.

Finding the admin department took for ever, even with the signs. Eleanor felt like a fish out of water as she wandered along the endless corridors, stunned at the traffic a busy hospital generated. A café for relatives as big as a restaurant in her town, a gift shop, a florist shop and endless people milling around—and apart from Eleanor they all seemed to know where they were going. Even the pay office seemed huge, a world away from the tiny room at the back of her beloved old hospital. And the bland face that stared back at her when she asked when her pay would be in, the dismissive shrug when they told her it wouldn't be for another fortnight, was, for Eleanor, the final straw.

*   *   *

'I thought you finished at four.' Pushing a cup of coffee towards her, Rory gave her a smile when finally she made it.

'I've been stuck in the pay office.'

'Hellhole.' Rory grimaced. 'Take it from someone who knows and email them next time. Far quicker than sitting in line for an hour just to be told they've mislaid your time sheet.'

'They didn't mislay it.' Eleanor's voice wiped the smile off his face and for the first time he noticed her red-rimmed eyes. 'Apparently I didn't hand it in on time. Where I worked before, you had up till midday on Monday.'

'It's nine a.m. here,' Rory said gently. 'Didn't anyone tell you?'

Eleanor shook her head. 'Which means that I've got to wait a fortnight now to be paid, which normally wouldn't matter…' Rolling her eyes, she managed a small smile. 'Well, it would, but it matters even more so now, given that I've just put up a bond and paid a month's rent in advance on a flat, and had all my worldly goods transported across the state…'

'Ouch.' Rory gave a sympathetic smile.

'Double ouch.' Eleanor's watery smile met his. 'All the stuff I swore I couldn't live without looked so impossibly grubby when it arrived and I pulled it out of the boxes. It would have been cheaper to buy it all new. Anyway,' she said crisply, changing the subject, 'we're not here to talk about my financial woes, just my harassment claim.'

It was worth it just to see his coffee slop into the saucer.

'That was a joke, by the way.'

'Glad to hear it.' His eyes met hers, a smile washing over his face, and somewhere between tipping the spilled coffee into the saucer and taking a grateful sip of his coffee, Eleanor wanted to make another joke. Not to lighten the atmosphere, not to show how witty she was, but to see that beautiful smile break out on that rugged face again, for those navy eyes to meet hers once more.

It was Eleanor struggling to keep her coffee in the cup now.

'I want to apologise to you for what happened in the drug room this morning. Mary was out of line,' Rory said finally, his voice unusually tentative, his eyes firmly on Eleanor, watching every flicker of her reaction. 'But, then again, Mary's often out of line, in the nicest possible way, of course. There's nothing remotely politically correct about her and, given that she's due for retirement in a couple of years, I'm not exactly holding my breath for any changes.

'However…' He took a deep breath, his eyes crinkling as he frowned for the longest moment, his lips poised as he debated his choice of words. When they came they were slow, measured and calm, but there was a sub-note Eleanor could hear, a sub-note that was riddled with mortification, and she cringed inside for Rory as he carried on talking. 'For Mary to suggest that the consultant of the department was somehow getting a kick out a young nurse treating him, well, it doesn't take Einstein to work out that even if it was meant as a joke, those sorts of comments can very easily be misconstrued.' He coughed, his eyes focusing now on his cooling coffee, his voice quieter, and Eleanor had to strain to catch it. 'And given your reaction this morning, clearly they were.'

'My overreaction this morning,' Eleanor said magnanimously, his discomfort so obvious, his apology so genuine, Eleanor knew it couldn't be anything other than from the heart. And she felt as if a great weight had been lifted from her shoulders, the entire morning's events given a new perspective now.

A glimpse that maybe things were going to be OK.

And not just on the career front!

That delicious rugby player she'd met was nudging his way back into view now, blending in beautifully with the dashing consultant that sat before her. It was a heady combination indeed.

'You had every right to be upset,' Rory continued, 'and if you'll allow me, I'll answer the question you asked this morning as best as I can.'

'What question?' Eleanor frowned.

'Why I let you shave my leg,' Rory reminded her.

'There's really no need.'

'There's every need, but first...' that delicious smile was there again, his hands rummaging in his suit pocket and pulling out some coins '...do you want anything from the vending machine?'

'Now, how could I refuse an offer like that, Mr Hunter?' Standing up, she followed him over to the machine, staring with a distinct lack of enthusiasm at the lonely yogurt twirling around next to a muffin on the revolving, refrigerated plates, the chocolate-chip cookie where the chocolate chip definitely remained in the singular and the woefully sad cracker selection with a sprig of parsley to try and cheer it up.

'Given the topic that we're discussing, would it be terribly foolhardy if I said there was a noodle bar two minutes up the road?'

'Probably,' Eleanor agreed, her mouth already watering and not just at the prospect of noodles. However, given that the single fifty-dollar note at the bottom of her bag was the only thing to feed her between now and next pay day, she at least managed to keep her response suitably tepid.

'And if I told you that it's on me, would that come across as pompous and chauvinist and mortally offend you?'

Another 'probably' was on the tip of her tongue, another cheeky smart-Alec reply ready to be delivered, but instead Eleanor swallowed it back. Rory was being kind and somehow Eleanor had a feeling it was par for the course with him. Turning shyly to him, she gave a small smile. 'Not at all,' she said softly. 'In fact, it would be lovely.'

The noodle bar was just that.

A row of Formica benches, with shiny metal stools you sat on while you waited for your order.

Apart from the two-minute kind, of which she was an expert, Eleanor had no idea what to choose and happily left the ordering to Rory, bagging a seat and watching as the world dashed around her. For the first time since she'd landed in Melbourne that nagging, nauseous, homesick feeling was put on hold and for a tiny slice of time it was fun just to be a spectator in a crowded café where no one knew anyone.

'Penny for them.' Placing a glass of wine in front of her, Rory made her jump as he squeezed onto the stool beside hers.

'Oh, they're worth more than that.' Grateful for the glass to fiddle with more than the drink, Eleanor sat quietly for a moment before she spoke. 'I was just thinking how different it is here. How no one actually

knows anyone. Back home you can't step out of the
front door without seeing a familiar face.'

'You miss it?'

Eleanor nodded. 'It probably sounds boring to you,
but it wasn't—it was nice. Most of the patients I
looked after I knew, not well, of course, but generally,
if you pushed hard enough there was some common
ground there—a daughter who'd been in my class, a
friend of my grandmother's…'

'It doesn't sound boring, it sounds nice,' Rory
mused, unscrewing the top of his beer.

'Most of the time, but, as nice as it can be, if you
don't get on with someone…' Taking a sip of her
wine, she gave a tight shrug. 'I had a few problems
in my old job.'

'What sort of problems?'

She'd been there before, had had this very conversation just a few nights ago, but Rory wasn't Pier.
Rory wasn't some intuitive gay agency nurse she was
working alongside for one night. Rory wasn't a sympathetic ally to grumble with in the pan room when
the going got a bit rough. Rory Hunter was the consultant of the department she'd just started to work
in, and if she had any hope of making it there, exposing her weaknesses would be a poor career move
indeed. So Eleanor chose her words rather more carefully than she had with Pier, looking Rory in the eye
and attempting to sound vaguely impartial.

'According to my manager, I didn't take my job
seriously enough.'

She didn't want to elaborate, would have loved to
have left it there, but Rory was frowning at her.

'That's not the impression I got. In fact I'd have

said it was the other way around. You seem very serious about your nursing.'

'I am!'

'So why would your manager say that?'

'She just did,' Eleanor answered irritably, but when his frown remained, when clearly evasiveness was going to get her nowhere, whether it was the wine or the navy eyes having an effect, Eleanor explained. 'According to my manager I was only using nursing as a stopgap.' He wasn't making this easy—in fact, had her glass not already been empty Eleanor would have taken a quick sip. 'Apparently, I was waiting for Mr Right to come along, or Dr Right,' Eleanor added with more than a trace of bitterness, 'or Paramedic Right. In fact, according to Rita anyone would have done.

'Do you see now why Mary's comment upset me so much? Rita, my old boss, would have said exactly the same and some more.'

'But why?'

'I've no idea,' Eleanor said wearily. 'For as long as I can remember I've wanted to be a nurse. The day I graduated was the happiest day of my life and even though the local country hospital mightn't be the cutting edge of nursing, it was the only place I wanted to be.' He watched as a smile lit up her pretty, strained face. 'I used to pass it on the way to school, I can even remember walking to Kinder and peering through the fence at the ambulance and the nurses in the white uniforms and I ached, ached to be part of it. It was all I ever wanted to be.'

'Then you should have stuck it out,' Rory responded. 'You should have told this Rita—'

'Don't you think I tried?' Eleanor cut in. 'And it

didn't make a scrap of difference. I told her the last thing on this earth I wanted right now was a husband and children. I was twenty-two, for heaven's sake…'

'You're twenty-two?' A slightly alarmed note in his voice made her smile.

'Twenty-three now,' Eleanor corrected as Rory took a very hefty swig of his beer, 'but, as I said over and over to Rita, I'm way too young to settle down. The last thing I need is a husband a mortgage and all that comes with it. I want to nurse.'

'So that's why you moved.'

Eleanor nodded. 'New start, new people. I could live with making a mistake on my first shift, even live with being a laughing stock for a while. But when Mary implied what she did this morning…' she gave another tight shrug '…I suppose she hit a nerve.'

'Mary often does.'

Eleanor just smiled.

'Do you regret coming here?' Rory asked softly, but Eleanor shook her head.

'My move wasn't all down to Rita. I'm not running away from anything. As my grad year rolled on I knew I needed more experience, knew that if I was going to be the emergency nurse I really wanted to be that at some point I'd need to move to the city. I guess Rita's attitude towards me just pushed things along a bit.'

'You'll certainly get experience here,' Rory mused. 'It's a busy department, too busy sometimes. It's not for everyone. This job can be incredibly stressful.'

Eleanor nodded. 'I can imagine and I can also see why the odd politically incorrect joke might be merited sometimes.'

'We'd all be sacked on the spot if the powers that

be heard us all carrying on at four a.m.,' Rory admitted. 'I'm glad you understand.'

'I'm appalled how far this has all come,' Eleanor continued. 'Where I come from, Mary Byrne's comment would have been one of many. I'm more than used to being relegated to a bimbo.' She gave a dry smile. 'Just look at me now, one week in and I've scored a date with the consultant.'

'Is that what you think?'

Eleanor shook her head. 'Of course not, but in my old life…' China-blue eyes dragged to his. 'I want a career, Rory. I want to be the best nurse I can be.'

'You will be,' Rory said assuredly, holding up his ticket as his number was called. 'Another wine?'

She should have put her hand over her glass and asked for a cola, but it was so nice to be spoiled, to be sitting in a crowded Melbourne café with Rory, and not to be home alone yet again. Another wine would be perfect!

It was hard not to look crestfallen when Rory appeared moments later with two tiny white boxes, balancing her glass of wine and a bottle of cola. Gorgeous boxes with silver handles they may be, but they'd both fit in her handbag with room to spare and Eleanor was starving.

Starving!

'You're not a vegetarian, are you?' Rory asked as she peered into her box. 'I should have checked.'

'Vegetarian? Is that one of those newfangled crazes everyone's going on about?'

His slightly startled expression only made her laugh.

'I'm a country girl, Rory. I could eat those beef noodles and the box and handle along with them.'

'They hold a lot,' Rory countered.

'They'd need to!' Flicking her eyes over his cola, she took an apologetic sip of her wine. 'Sorry, I didn't realise you were on call.'

'I'm not.' Rory shrugged. 'And if the truth be known, another beer would go down well with chili beef noodles but no doubt someone will page me, sooner rather than later.'

'When you're not on call?' Eleanor frowned up at him. 'Surely you're entitled to a night off.'

'I'd rather the staff rang if there was a problem,' Rory answered, his easy tones turning dry. 'And at Melbourne Central there's always a problem. It's no big deal.' Those massive, tense shoulders shrugged a couple of inches. 'If I was sick I'd want me there.'

And it should have sounded conceited. Coming from anyone else it would have sounded utterly ostentatious, but again those eyes were staring at her, honesty shining like a prism, and all Eleanor could do was stare back.

Stare back and try to ignore the image of a pot of gold at the end of this forbidden rainbow.

He disappeared off to the loo, leaving Eleanor to play with her chopsticks, mulling over the turn of events that had landed her here with the most divine, out-of-bounds man in history. A furious abacus clicked in her head as she worked out the mean age of a consultant but, no matter which way she looked at it or the allowances she made for her appalling maths, unless Rory Hunter had been a child genius, the man who'd disappeared for a moment was easily a decade older than her.

And some more.

'So why did you let me shave you?' He'd barely

sat down before she'd blurted the words out. 'I mean, after all, that's why we're here, isn't it?'

'Indeed.'

Wow, he was good with chopsticks, those massive hands nimbly working the box as Eleanor fumbled on with hers.

'Despite your first opinion, I wasn't drunk.'

Her dubious stare made it clear she begged to differ, but Rory's response was pure indignation. 'I wasn't. However, we had just won a shield and a cherished one, too. The Koo-Wee-Rup guys have had it for years, you've no idea how good it felt finally…' Her glazed expression stalled him. 'I'm boring you.'

'Totally,' Eleanor agreed. 'My brothers play Australian Rules football. Actually, they don't play it, they live it, Monday to Sunday, and it's all they talk about.'

'Sorry.'

'Don't be.' Digging into her noodles, Eleanor waved with her free hand. 'I'm an expert at feigning interest where sport's concerned. So tell me again, the Koo-Wee-Rup guys…'

'I'd had a good drink,' Rory broke in, each word tinged with a hint of regret. 'An extremely well-deserved one, I might add.'

She was working those noodles, scarcely able to believe she'd been eating nonstop for ten minutes and the box was still full.

'But I wasn't drunk.'

'I know,' Eleanor admitted. 'I didn't at the time and thank heavens I took Sister Byrne's advice and refrained from writing my opinion in your notes. But as appealing as your sobriety might be, from where I'm sitting that gives you even less of an excuse to hide behind, even less of an excuse for letting some idiot walk up and shave your leg.' She was smiling now, the brittle wariness of the morning completely gone now, absolutely comfortable in his presence, glad, so glad that someone in the world actually if not understood then seemed vaguely receptive to her rather dry, offbeat humour. 'So come on, then, why did you let me shave you?'

'You seemed so sure you were doing it right.'

A tiny laughed escaped her lips. 'You're a consultant, Rory. Surely you of all people could have pointed out that I wasn't doing it right, that I was doing it horribly wrong.'

'I didn't want to pull rank.'

His admission stilled her. For a while there, had she known the slightest thing about rugby she'd been running with ball, slightly elated, for once on top of things, but suddenly the ref had blown his whistle, suddenly she'd been called offside for a reason she couldn't begin to fathom.

'I didn't want to say to this nurse, who was doing her best, who seemed so sure, that I was a consultant and would she, please, send in the sister in charge. And on top of that,' Rory continued as Eleanor just gaped back, 'the last thing I needed, the very last thing I wanted, though if you ever quote me I'll firmly deny it, never in a million years did I want Mary Byrne fussing over me like a broody hen and telling me she had four strapping lads just like me back home and not to worry if I had a drink on board, that, sure, I was the consultant, but didn't everyone deserve a day off?' His imitation of Mary's accent was so spot on, if his expression hadn't been so serious Eleanor would have laughed. 'So when what I thought was an agency nurse burst in and took over, I was more than happy to hand over the reins to someone I assumed I'd never see again, more than happy to get the hell out of the department when she practically ordered me to leave. Can you understand that?'

'I think so.'

'Eleanor, I work six days out of seven and most of those nights I'm on call with a pager by the bed and a brain that can't fully switch off just in case I'm needed. Tossing a ball around once a week is about the only time I escape, the only time I'm not Mr Hunter or someone's boss, just another ugly guy covered in mud. The very last place I wanted to be that Saturday night was in my own department, slightly the worse for wear with Mary Byrne assuring me it would go no further.' He gave a wry smile. 'And the best part of it is, your shaving worked like a dream.' When she stared back at him open-mouthed he nodded. 'It stayed on for three days, Eleanor. A bit of cling film in the shower and the blessed thing stayed on. I'm telling you, if everyone in the department wouldn't fall about laughing I'd be prescribing shaved limbs and sticky plaster for every deep laceration—it actually worked. It didn't have a thing to do with you and everything to do with me.'

'And you really didn't recognise me this morning?'

He shook his head and she gave a wan smile, flicking her eyes down to her noodle box which still seemed inordinately full. 'They should call this place ''never-ending noodles''.'

'Told you there'd be plenty.'

'More than plenty!' Tucking the lid closed, Eleanor picked up her box. 'There's enough here for my dinner tomorrow night.'

'And the next couple of nights.' Rory grinned as a waiter deposited another box on their table. 'I ordered some more for you,' he explained. 'You seemed so sure you'd finish them.'

'That's me.' Eleanor grinned. '"Positively wrong" should be my middle name.'

'Please, don't say anything more to Mary.' They were strolling down Elizabeth Street now, heading back towards the hospital, trams clattering past as a bosky dusk descended, Eleanor clutching her boxes of noodles, and for all the world it felt as if the evening should only just be starting.

'I don't want to,' Rory admitted. 'As grating as she can be sometimes, I wouldn't change a hair on her head. Mary's always saying, "You'll miss me when I'm gone." Firmly tongue in cheek, of course. And I always counter it with, "No one's indispensable, Mary, not even you." But the truth of the matter is, that place is going to miss her when she finally goes. There's still a lot to be said for the old-school nurses.'

'I know what you mean,' Eleanor murmured. 'Sometimes I wish I'd been born a hundred years ago—you know, when nurses wore those hats and buckles and lived in the residences, when there was an ogre of a matron bearing down on you.' Smiling up at him, she explained further. 'It just seemed more cut and dried then. Nurses were nurses, that was what they did, that was all they wanted to do. Don't get me wrong,' Eleanor added, remembering that this was her boss after all. 'I'm all for extended roles. I can't wait to put in IVs and go out with the paramedics on a ride-along, I can't wait to learn to intubate people, it's just…'

'Just what?'

'It doesn't leave much time for talking to the patients, does it?'

'And you're very good at that.' They were at the hospital now, lights blazing from a thousand windows, a small city in itself. 'Where are you parked?'

'A long way from here.' Eleanor smiled up at him. 'My car would have fared the transition to the city even worse than me, I'm afraid. My brothers are supposed to be selling it for me.'

'I'll give you a lift, then,' Rory offered.

'No need, I'm only over there.' She pointed to a rather grubby-looking block of flats. 'Don't worry, it's worse than it looks.'

'I'll walk you over.'

'No need,' Eleanor said, too lightly. 'I do it every night.' She'd have loved to have asked him in, would have loved to be one of those cool sophisticates who casually smiled as they suggested coming up for a coffee.

But quite simply she couldn't, so instead she settled for a small shrug.

'Thanks for the noodles. If pay day ever comes, I'll return the treat.'

'Eleanor?' She was turning for the road now, possibly heading straight into the path of an oncoming tram, but anywhere would be preferable to standing on a street corner and attempting a casual goodnight to a man as overtly sexy as Rory Hunter. 'Why don't you let me—?'

'Please, don't.' Holding up her noodle-boxed hand, Eleanor cut him off in mid-sentence. 'Please, don't spoil a lovely evening by offering me a loan. I'm really not the poor little waif I make out. Once the bank gets its backside into gear and transfers my funds over, and once the pay office actually acknowledges that I exist, no doubt, I'll be dining out at the noodle bar every night of the week.'

'If you won't let me give you a loan, can I at least talk to the pay office on your behalf?' When she didn't answer he rattled on quickly, determined to have his say without giving offence. 'They could draw a cheque, make an offline payment maybe. If I get on their backs I'm sure they'll manage something.'

Again a smart reply bobbed on her tongue.

Again she swallowed it.

'That would be great.'

Thankfully a tram wasn't coming. Very thankfully as it turned out, for Eleanor looked neither left nor right, just crossed the road as if she were walking on water and travelled up in the creaking lift as if she were floating on air. Depositing her precious cargo in the fridge, she screwed her nose up at the cheap cask wine Rory probably wouldn't deign to gargle with and sniffed at the very questionable milk, before tipping it down the sink, thankful she hadn't asked him in. Staring at her tiny lounge room, Eleanor's heart sank ever further. The jumble of cheap cane furniture her mother had donated from the summer room, the poster on the wall that had looked so cheerful in her bedroom at home, here they just looked…

Pathetic.

Eyeing the room critically Eleanor took in every glossy magazine, every coffee-cup that littered every surface, the endless piles of CDs, the make-up bag spilling its contents, every last item ramming home the gaping years and lifestyles that separated them.

Picking her way through the debris, she crossed the room and leant her burning cheeks against the cool window, gazing across at the hospital she was now a part of, watching in awe as a chopper hovered like an angry bee above the massive building, her excitement mounting as the thudding noise of the rotors filtered through her windows and wondering over and over how one casual meal, one lazy smile could render this vast city almost home.

CHAPTER FOUR

IT WAS a slightly awkward Eleanor that arrived at the nurses' station the following morning, only this time it had nothing to do with the mistake she had made on her first night and everything to do with the recipient.

It was no big deal, Eleanor reminded herself firmly, just a box of noodles and an off-the-record chat. Rory had probably headed for home with no more than a sense of relief that a problem had been averted.

It wouldn't even have entered his head that he may have just caused a bigger one.

And it would be a problem, Eleanor told herself, a twenty-three-year-old junior nurse with a king-size crush on a consultant was the last thing he needed. And it was a crush. Eleanor's mental scolding grew louder inside her head as she idly watched him scribbling some notes up at the nurses' station, dressed in theatre blues, a shadow dusting his jaw, eyes fanning at the sides as they did when he concentrated, hunched over the paperwork, those massive shoulders strung with tension.

A delayed teenage crush for a man who'd been nice when she'd been feeling down.

Maybe he felt her watching him, maybe he was just taking a break from his notes, but suddenly he looked up, those dark eyes smiling momentarily as he caught her watching him.

'Sister Lewis.' Mary's voice was crude intrusion.

'Would you mind checking the drugs with me this morning?'

Eleanor nodded and followed but she frowned at Mary's back as they walked to the drug room. Mary had just checked the drugs with the night shift. On every shift change a registered nurse counted the controlled drugs before handing over the keys, and there was no reason, no reason at all for Mary to count them again, at least none that Eleanor could see.

'You're wondering why I've asked you here?' After the longest silence Mary finally spoke. 'Given that I've just checked the drugs.'

'A bit,' Eleanor admitted, frowning at Mary's darkening cheeks, surprised to see the normally confident older woman for once struggling for eloquence.

'It's the one place in the department you can guarantee no one's going to overhear,' Mary explained, fiddling with the keys in her hand. 'The ideal place to apologise in private.'

'Apologise?'

Mary nodded. 'Rory and I had a little talk yesterday. Actually, that's a lie. Rory spoke and I listened. All night I've been going over and over what I said…' Her face was purple when finally she looked up and Eleanor felt a huge surge of sympathy for the other woman as Mary fumbled on. 'It was a joke, a silly joke, and not for a single moment did I mean it. Rory says that's no excuse that I should know better, but that's me all over, the words are out before I've thought things through. I should have held my tongue, should never have implied—'

'Mary,' Eleanor broke in, smiling gently back at her senior. 'Please, don't hold your tongue on my account. As you said, it was a joke, a throw-away

comment that on any other day I'd have probably
found funny.'

'Well, it's very nice of you to say that but, like it
or not, I do need to change my ways a bit. Nursing
has moved on, Eleanor. It's not just about patients,
it's not just about doing the right thing by people any
more, it's about being *seen* to do the right thing.
Careless talk has no place in an emergency department these days, which is a shame. Sometimes a bit
of humour, however inappropriate, can be what it
takes to see you through.

'Now!' Her tone changed, back to the bossy, efficient charge nurse Eleanor was starting to actually
like. 'How about you do the hand clinic this morning?'

'With Vicki?' Eleanor checked, but Mary shook
her head.

'I'm sure you can manage the hand clinic on your
own. You'd have done them in the country?' When
Eleanor nodded she gave a brief smile. 'I'll send a
student around to give you a hand.'

Her own student!

Glowing with excitement, Eleanor raced to
Reception, determined that this would be the most
efficient, most organised hand clinic Melbourne
Central had ever seen. Her confidence wavered
slightly when the receptionist handed her a stack of
cards.

'Busy clinic this morning.'

'There must be thirty cards here,' Eleanor groaned.

'And the patients are already starting to arrive.
Don't forget to take the X-rays with you.'

Where Eleanor had worked, the hand clinic had
consisted of three, possibly five patients. Most hand

injuries were called back the next day to check for signs of infection and mobility. Eleanor had a fair idea of what it entailed—but thirty of them!

'Sister Lewis?' A terrified-looking nurse greeted her as Eleanor walked into the empty clinic room. 'I'm Student Nurse Jacobs. Sister Byrne said I was to give you a hand.'

'I've already got thirty to deal with.' Eleanor grinned, but changed track when Nurse Jacobs didn't respond to her small joke. 'I'm Eleanor. What's your first name?'

'Amanda.'

'And have you ever done a hand clinic, Amanda?'

'No, I haven't really done anything. It's only my second day in Emergency.'

'It's only my second week,' Eleanor admitted openly. 'But don't worry about a thing, we'll get through.' Pulling out the first card, Eleanor went through it with Amanda. 'DD. Normally it stands for dry dressing, but when it's put next to a follow-up appointment it's usually shorthand for dressing down. Basically the doctor wants the dressing taken down before he sees the patient. Now, sometimes it can take a while to get them off, so where I used to work, to make things run smoothly we used to start taking them down before the clinic actually started. I assume it's the same here so we should start calling people in shortly. Anyone whose dressing is sticking, set up a dressing pack and squirt the wound with saline, let it soak for a while and once the dressing comes off easily, cover it with some clean gauze and send them back in line.'

'You make it sound so easy,' Amanda mumbled.

'It is,' Eleanor said with an assured air of confidence that didn't quite match how she really felt. 'Come on, I'll show you.'

And show her Eleanor did, bringing the patients in and gently taking dressings down, chatting amicably about their injuries and how they had occurred, watching with quiet satisfaction as Amanda finally bit the bullet and called a patient through for herself.

'It's sticking.'

'Then give it another squirt of saline,' Eleanor said patiently, smiling at the teenager whose hand was on the trolley. 'That's right. See how it comes away easily. Now, put some gauze on and tell your patient to go back to the waiting room. It shouldn't be long now,' Eleanor added to the patient.

'Eleanor.' Mary bustled in. 'Mr Hunter will be round in just a moment, I meant to show you how he likes to have his table laid up for the clinic.' Pulling out pads, she laid them in line and pointed to each in turn. 'Sick certificates, prescription pad, X-Ray referrals, all the usual. Now, Mr Hunter doesn't generally make a fuss as to what order they're in so long as he's got them to hand, but some of the consultants like them to be arranged just so. There's a pad in the top drawer, outlining their preferences for the various clinics.

'Right.' Catching her breath, she nodded to Eleanor. 'Maybe you should bring the first couple in and start soaking off their dressings. Here's Mr Hunter now.'

'Morning, ladies.' The theatre blues had gone. The hour or so since she'd seen him last must have been taken up with a shave and a shower, for Rory looked every bit the smooth, suave consultant and nothing like the tired, overworked doctor she'd seen only a short while before.

'Come on, Eleanor,' Mary gently scolded. 'You need to get things moving.'

'I've already soaked their dressing off,' Eleanor answered.

'Well, bring the next lot in.'

'I've done them—I mean, *we've* done them,' Eleanor corrected, smiling over at Amanda.

'You mean all the dressings are off?' Wide-eyed, she turned to Rory. 'Looks like it will be a speedy clinic this morning.'

'Suits me.' Rory grinned, picking up the wad of cards. 'I might even make it to the canteen for last breakfast. Now, Eleanor, did Mary explain that I was doing a drug trial?'

'Oh, Rory,' Mary apologised, 'I completely forgot about it.'

'No problem,' Rory replied easily, unclipping a rather large metal case and waving Amanda and Eleanor over. 'You get on, Mary, I'll explain what I'm doing.' Opening the case, he pulled out a pile of paperwork, exposing row after row of white bottles. 'It's a blind trial. Do either of you know what that means?'

'No idea,' Amanda admitted, but Eleanor chewed on her lip for a thoughtful moment before answering.

'Is that where you don't know what drug you're giving?'

'Correct.' Rory gave an encouraging nod. 'Some of these tablets are a standard, regular antibiotic that I usually prescribe for infected wounds while the others are the new drug which is being trialled. With the patients' consent I'll give them a full course of antibiotics and then carefully monitor their progress, documenting all my findings. Once the trial is finished, all the notes are sent back to be collaborated.'

'Do you find out then what you were prescribing?' Eleanor asked, picking up one of the white bottles and staring at the row of numbers.

'Not individually, but I'll get back a courtesy report on the data.'

'And you really have no idea when you prescribe it whether it's the new drug you're giving or the old faithful?'

'None. Though this is an approved trial, the drugs are very safe. The main thing I need you two to know is that if the patients have any questions about the trial, refer them straight back to me. It's very important that patients are fully informed about these trials. Even if the question seems pretty straightforward, just pass it on to me. It's very good of the patients to participate in this sort of trial so the very least they deserve is an answer to any questions.

'Right, send the first one in.'

Eleanor did as he'd asked. In fact, Eleanor did as he asked for the best part of two hours, not that Rory ordered her around, just diligently wrote up his notes, occasionally outlining a certain treatment, but every request, every question was followed up with a polite murmur of thanks. Even Amanda seemed to relax, working hard, happy to defer to Eleanor anything she didn't understand, remembering to call Rory when one of the trial patients asked a question as she dealt with his dressing.

And even though a hand clinic might not be the front line of Emergency, even though no lives had been saved, no heroics done, Eleanor revelled in her morning. Her confidence mounted with every patient who was seen and sent home, and she found out that not only was it a bit of an ego boost to have a student under her, she actually enjoyed teaching. But even more inspiring, Eleanor realised that morning that though she had a lot to learn, she also wasn't a complete novice. Those three years of training and her grad year combined had left her with some solid foundations on which to build.

'Great, ladies.' Throwing his pen down, Rory stretched long arms above his head and yawned loudly, not even bothering to cover it now every last patient had finally gone. 'The clinic went really well.'

'Honestly,' Eleanor checked. 'You're not just being nice?'

'Eleanor,' Rory sighed, 'why would I say that the clinic went well if it didn't?'

Eleanor shrugged. 'To be polite?'

'I've been here for most of the night,' Rory pointed out. 'Believe me, I'm beyond being polite for the sake of it. If the clinic had bombed I'd have told you in no uncertain terms.'

'So I did OK?'

He rolled his eyes, but she could tell he was smiling.

'You were great, Eleanor. Do you want me to put it in writing?'

'I might hold you to that.' Eleanor grinned, pulling over a trolley and starting to clean it, prolonging the conversation without even a second thought. 'What time did you get called in last night?' she asked, wiping down the trolleys as she spoke.

'Two a.m.' Clasping his hands behind his head, he yawned again. 'But I don't want to be reminded of that, given I've only had two hours' sleep and there's still a full day ahead of me. Now, as nice as it is to chat, I really ought to get on.

'Why do I do these trials?' he murmured, salvaging his pen and staring at the mountain of paperwork in front of him. 'Now I've got to fill in all these sheets.'

'Do they pay you?' She wasn't being nosy, just interested, but Rory's lips twitched into a smile at her forthrightness before he answered.

'Do you mean, will I be on a cruise ship heading for the Caribbean some time next month? In a word, no. The best the drug rep will rustle up is yet another mouse for my computer and, no doubt, a multitude of pens.' Rummaging in his pocket, he handed her one, watching as Eleanor stared at it. And very nice it was, too, a fluorescent purple gel pen with the drug company's name emblazoned on the side, but not much to show for the hours of work the trial would undoubtedly entail.

'Keep it.' Rory grinned as Eleanor signed her name on a scrap piece of paper.

'But it's yours.'

'They gave me a box.'

'Can I have one for Amanda, then?'

'Here.' Pulling another one out of his pocket, he handed it over. 'I've got an endless supply. You never know, though, when the trial ends and they come for the data, the reps might surprise us and put on a cheese and fruit platter in the staffroom.'

'So why do you do it, then?' Eleanor asked. 'Why take on all the extra work when you've clearly got enough to contend with and you don't get anything in return?'

'Well, it's interesting, I suppose.'

Eleanor screwed up her nose and Rory laughed.

'Maybe I'm just boring.'

'I don't think so.' It was an entirely innocent response to a joky comment, so why, then, was the colour mounting on her cheeks? Why, then, was she suddenly taking great interest in buffing her stainless-steel trolley to a dazzling sheen?

'I'd better get on.' This time when he picked up his pen Rory clearly meant business. 'Thanks again, ladies,' he called as they headed out of the clinic.

Turning, Eleanor caught sight of him, hunched over the desk, staring at his pile of notes, and the response he evoked had nothing to do with the fact that he looked so dammed gorgeous, nothing to do with the fact that just the sight of him caused her breath to catch in her throat, and everything to do with the fact that now that the patients had gone, now he could relax and finally be just Rory, he looked so dog tired, so snowed under that Eleanor paused in the doorway, battling with a sudden influx of nerves.

'Can I bring you a coffee?'

'Best offer I've had all day.'

His smile was worth her blush.

'Two sugars, and strong enough to stand the spoon in.'

Which probably wasn't very good for him, but Eleanor did as he'd asked and even found a couple of biscuits then carried them carefully back to him, placing them on the desk beside him without saying a word, before quietly turning to go.

'Oh, Eleanor?' He called her back. 'I didn't want to give you this in front of everyone.' Digging in his pocket, he pulled out an envelope and handed it to her. 'Hopefully this will make things easier for you.'

Mortified she pushed it back. 'I told you, Rory, I don't want a loan.'

'It isn't a loan,' Rory responded. 'In fact, you've earned every last cent of it. I had the pay roll manager draw you a cheque. It took a hell of a lot of persuading, mind.'

'They paid me.' A delighted grin split her face as she ripped open the envelope. 'But they told me there was absolutely nothing they could do, that I'd have to wait for the next pay run…'

'And I told them that if they didn't get their backsides into gear, Melbourne Central's latest acquisition would be hotfooting it back to the country.' He gave a small wink. 'Sometimes you have to bend the facts a bit to get what you want in life.'

'Thank you,' Eleanor said breathlessly. 'You've no idea the difference this will make to me. Thank you,' she said again, but Rory waved her away.

'It's no big deal.' Turning back to his notes, he set back to work, only this time as she reached the door it was Rory who called her back, Rory now prolonging the conversation.

'I enjoyed talking to you last night, Eleanor.'

From across the clinic she couldn't quite read his expression but there was a tension in the air, a subtle undercurrent that surely couldn't just be emanating from her!

'I enjoyed it, too.' Not the wittiest of responses but it was the best Eleanor could do.

'We should do it again some time?'

She heard a question in his voice and nodded dumbly, terrified to speak in case he heard the tremor that would surely be in her voice.

Picking up his pen and getting back to his notes,

he effectively dismissed her and for a tiny stolen moment she stood there, glued to the spot, scarcely able to comprehend what had surely just happened.

Had Rory Hunter just asked her out?

CHAPTER FIVE

'I'VE got a child I'd like to bring over to Resus, Mary.' Walking over to her senior, Eleanor stood quietly as Mary worked on, not remotely offended when Mary didn't immediately answer, instead concentrating on keeping her face impassive as she looked at the injuries of the screaming child she was working on. His small body was covered in angry red burns and Mary poured sterile water over drapes, the paediatric registrar attempted to put in a second IV line to push fluids through, dehydration a dangerous consequence of burns. The registrar's glasses slipped to the end of her nose and after only the slightest hesitation Eleanor pushed them up for her, neither expecting nor receiving thanks, the little life that hung in the balance the sole focus of attention right now.

'The anaesthetist is coming down.' Mary addressed the registrar first. 'He can try to get another line in. Now, Eleanor, who's the child you want brought over?'

'Marcus Kane,' Eleanor started, 'an eighteen-month-old asthmatic. He was here a few weeks ago…'

'I just saw him,' the registrar broke in. 'What's happened?'

'Nothing.' Eleanor swallowed, trying to voice what she couldn't really fathom herself.

Marcus had been in the department two hours now and his condition hadn't improved. Regular nebulisers had done nothing to alleviate his wheeze, and although he was still smiling, still interested in the book his patient father was reading to him, something wasn't right. 'I've just given him another Ventolin and Atrovent nebuliser but there's still no improvement.'

'What are his sats doing?' the registrar asked.

'Still ninety-five per cent,' Eleanor answered, 'but that's on forty per cent oxygen. He's using his accessory muscles. I think he's becoming exhausted and needs to be over in Resus.'

'Where?'

Mary had a point. Every trolley was full with dangerously ill patients, all the senior nurses and doctors stretched to the limit. The late shift that had started so quietly for Eleanor clearly wasn't going to end in the same vein. Marcus had been in the process of being examined by the paediatric registrar when the burns child had been rushed in, and though his condition hadn't deteriorated Eleanor had an uneasy feeling it was about to.

'Put him on continuous Ventolin,' the registrar ordered, turning to her intern. 'Dale, go and have another listen to his chest and I'll be out to him just as soon as—'

'Doctor.' Mary's voice commanded the registrar's instant attention. The alarms were starting to bleep in loud urgency as the burns child's blood pressure plummeted. Mary instantly wound the head of the trolley down as the child's screaming went ominously quiet. She reached for an ambu-bag. 'Eleanor, put out an emergency page for the anaesthetist.'

Dashing to the phone, Eleanor watched her trembling finger punch in the emergency number, relaying

Mary's orders then swiftly making her way back, the overhead loudspeaker springing into life, and Eleanor knew there and then that Dale wasn't going to be coming out to listen to Marcus's chest any time in the next few minutes, that Mary was stretched to the utter limit, handling a burns victim as other nurses worked on with their equally precarious charges. She could hear Vicki's raised voice from behind a curtain, calling to someone to alert Theatre, see Pier's usually smiling face set in grim concentration as he eyed a cardiac monitor on the other side of the room with the emergency registrar, his patient an unhealthy grey. It was at that precise moment that Eleanor grew up.

The adolescent stage of nursing was over now.

She'd been there a month, had, as Mary insisted, run everything by her senior, had hardly coughed without asking first. But Mary was busy now and if ever there was a time to put her skills to use, to become an effective member of the team, now was the time.

'Eleanor,' Mary called to her as she headed for the door, 'can you deal with it?'

It wasn't an order, it was a question, and she gave an appreciative small smile as after only the tiniest hesitation Eleanor nodded.

'I'll keep you informed.'

'He's getting worse!' Marcus's father was running towards her, panic in his eyes. 'I mean he's still smiling, still…'

Eleanor made her way briskly over, listening to the child's chest with her stethoscope, the wheeze still ominously present. Pulling the prongs out of her ears, she filled the nebule with Ventolin, smiling reassuringly at the child's father. 'We're going to give this to him continuously now. I'm just going to make a call and I'll be right back. Press this if you need me.'

I'd rather the staff rang me if there was a problem.

Rory's words echoed in her mind as she asked the switchboard to connect her. If there had been time she would have loved to have checked with Mary or run it by Dr Patel, the emergency registrar, who was on this evening, but there wasn't time, Eleanor thought grimly.

More hands were needed.

'Putting you through to his mobile now.' The elderly voice of the switchboard operator was replaced in a second by a younger, rather huskier one.

'Rory Hunter's phone.'

'It's Sister Lewis calling from Melbourne Central. May I speak to him, please?'

She could hear the exasperated sigh of the woman, hear the clinking of glasses, the drone of chatter in the background, and Eleanor closed her eyes for a second, questioning for the first time the wisdom behind calling him, but there was no time for introspection as his crisp voice came over the line.

'Eleanor!'

'Sorry,' she said. 'I know you're not on call...'

'Problem?' His voice was clipped, a contrast to her rather nervous chatter, and Eleanor cleared her throat and assumed a rather more professional tone.

'It's exceptionally busy. Resus is full, the anaesthetist and paediatricians are with a burns child and the second anaesthetist is setting up for a ruptured aortic aneurysm that Vicki's about to take up to Theatre. I have an eighteen-month-old with asthma who doesn't seem to be improving. His sats are ninety-five per cent on forty per cent—'

'I'm walking to my car now,' Rory broke in. 'Stay with him and give continuous Ventolin.'

'That's what I'm doing,' Eleanor responded. 'Look, Rory, maybe you don't need to come in. He's not flat, he's not going off, maybe I'm wrong…'

'Let's hope so.' He didn't comment further, just rang off, and Eleanor set to work. Pulling a crash cart over, she placed red dots on Marcus and connected him to a cardiac monitor, all the while chatting in reassuring tones to Marcus and his father.

'Some of the medications Marcus might need will require him to be monitored more closely,' she explained as she set up the equipment, attaching a tiny blood-pressure cuff to his arm. 'And as the high-dependency area,' Eleanor said, deliberately avoiding the word resuscitation, 'is very full and very noisy, we're going to keep him here. He needs to be kept calm, so just keep right on reading to him and talking to him while I work on. Mr Hunter, the consultant, will be here shortly.'

'How are we doing?' Mary was dashing over, her face concerned, eyeing the equipment Eleanor was setting up without comment.

'We're fine,' Eleanor responded, smiling at Marcus's father. 'I rang Mr Hunter and he's on his way in.'

She waited for a horrified look from Mary, for that caustic tongue to deliver a comment for Eleanor's ears only, that she'd overstepped that mark, but instead Mary gave a brief nod, listening to the child's chest through a stethoscope before addressing the father.

'He's better off here at the moment,' Mary said, 'believe me.'

'Sister explained.' Marcus's father gave a worried nod. 'But what if he gets worse?'

'Then Sister will bring him directly over. We can make room for him, that's not the issue. The issue is keeping this little boy calm and reassured.' She gave a small nod. 'Which is what's happening. Right, sister. I can see you've got everything under control. My patient is going up to ICU shortly.' She pulled out a flask and a box of aminophylline from the crash trolley. 'Maybe you could start pulling that up while you're waiting for Mr Hunter. Don't add it till he's calculated the dose, just get everything ready. Any problems in the meantime, press the bell three times. Vicki's running a patient to Theatre. As soon as she's back I'll send her over to you.' A relieved smile lit up her knowing face. 'Here's Mr Hunter now.'

Here he was indeed.

Dressed in a dinner suit, his hair slicked back, he made his way directly over. Eleanor turned, expecting Mary to give him a brief handover, but she was dashing back to Resus and finally Eleanor knew she was in.

That Mary trusted her.

'Thanks for coming in.' There was no place for apologies now. The judgement call had been made. 'He's still holding his own.'

'He's tired, though.' Gently Rory examined the child, listening to his chest and examining his X-ray film then writing the IV orders, which Eleanor had dutifully drawn up. 'Any ICU beds?'

'None. Well, there were two, but the burns child's

going up soon and I think the other one's being held
for the aneurysm that's just gone to Theatre.'

'It is,' Vicki said somewhat breathlessly as she
came over.

'We'll see about that,' Rory muttered. 'I'm just going to make a call. The continuous Ventolin's helping
and the aminophylline will kick in very soon.' He
nodded to Vicki and Eleanor. 'I'm just popping to the
staffroom to make a call. I'll be right back.'

He stalked off and Vicki gave a small giggle, wink-
ing at the little boy who managed a tired smile back,
thankfully looking a touch better now. Eleanor wished
she could be as effortlessly reassuring as Vicki, as
relaxed with all the monitors and equipment that
buzzed around this little boy as she was.

'He needs intensive care?' Marcus's father was so
pale he looked as if he might faint. 'Are they going
to put him on a ventilator or something?'

'Nothing like that,' Vicki soothed. 'He just needs
to be monitored very closely at the moment and
there's simply not enough staff on the children's ward
to do that. If a child requires nebulisers this frequently
then the policy is that we send them to ICU.'

She was good. Eleanor listened to Vicki closely,
smiling when Vicki turned her attention to Eleanor.
'We're all under control here and Resus is much more
settled now. Why don't you head off to the staffroom
and grab a quick coffee? You haven't had a break
yet, you must be gasping.'

'I'm fine,' Eleanor said. 'Anyway, the night staff
will be here soon.'

But Vicki was insistent. 'Go, and while you're
there you'll find out more about hospital policies and
the politics behind them in the five minutes than you

will from any of the manuals we're expected to read.'
She grinned at Eleanor's bemused expression. 'How
to create an ICU bed out of thin air. Go on.' She
grinned. 'You'll learn heaps.'

Again Vicki was right. Even before Eleanor walked
into the staffroom, clutching a very welcome coffee,
she could feel the walls shaking as Rory roared, lit-
erally roared into the telephone.

'So you're telling me that you're holding the only
ICU bed for a patient who at best is going to be in
Theatre and Recovery for at least another six hours,
when I've got a baby down here requiring an aminophylline infusion and continuous Ventolin who
needs intensive care now?'

Eleanor actually felt sorry for whoever was on the
other end of the line because whatever their response
was, it clearly was the wrong one.

'I don't care what sort of shuffling has to be done.
Frankly, I don't care if you have to call in extra staff
and keep the patient in Recovery. You should see the
shuffling that's had to go on here. At least the ICU
staff are getting fifteen minutes' notice. What notice,
apart from a blue light, do we get here?' He turned
then, seeing Eleanor sitting there gulping her coffee,
and she was amazed that someone so apparently livid
could give such a gorgeous smile and nod as he carried on shouting into the phone. 'Yes, fifteen minutes'
notice. You heard right, and I'm bringing him up myself.'

Slamming down the phone, he again gave her the
benefit of another very nice smile. 'You can see why
I choose to do this out of earshot of the father.'

'Absolutely,' Eleanor agreed, praying for a flash of

inspiration, for a witty response to fly from her lips, settling instead for another sip of coffee.

'Well, enjoy your break. I'd better give ICU a quick courtesy call and tell them we're on our way. Their fifteen minutes will soon be up.'

She nodded to his departing back, appalled how pleased she felt just to see him, to hear him, the whole shift made more special just because Rory Hunter was near.

'Get a grip, Eleanor,' she scolded herself aloud, gulping down the hot sweet drink then heading back to Emergency, smiling at Mr Kane and Vicki as she came over.

'He'll be going up shortly.'

'Amazing what a bit of brawn can do, isn't it?' Vicki winked again, fiddling with the oxygen.

'He looks a lot more settled.'

'He is,' Vicki agreed. 'His sats are ninety-seven on thirty-five per cent now and see how his rib retraction is a bit less marked? He's going to be fine.'

'Ready for the off?' Mary appeared, looking a lot more relaxed. 'Mr Hunter is coming to take him up now.'

'Can I take him?' Vicki asked. 'I'd like to pop my head around the door of the relatives' room and see how my patient's relatives are doing.'

'I'm sure Eleanor won't mind.' Mary smiled. 'In fact, Eleanor, why don't you go home? The night staff are arriving. I'm sure you've got other places you'd rather be.'

But Eleanor did mind. She minded very much.

Heading for the staffroom and picking up her bag, Eleanor knew she should be pleased. OK, Mary had only let her leave half an hour early, but she knew it was actually an affirmation, a quiet nod of approval from her senior that tonight she had worked well. And naturally Vicki had every reason to want to head back up to ICU, but Eleanor had wanted to be the one to go.

Wanted to be the one walking swiftly alongside Rory and handing over their small charge and, who knew, walking back to Emergency rather more slowly.

She fiddled with her hair for ages, chatted to the arriving night staff, even stopped at the vending machine for a bar of chocolate before heading across the ambulance bay, trying desperately not to linger. The sound of Rory's footsteps behind her had every sense on high alert and when he called her name it was an effort to keep the joyous smile from her face as she swung round and feigned surprise.

'Rory! How is he?'

'In the right place.' He gave a small smile. 'I know it can't have been easy for you tonight to call me. I spoke to Mary and she told me just how busy the place got, how you made the decision yourself.

'It was the right one,' he added, and Eleanor gave a tiny wince.

'Just as well.'

'Don't even start to think like that.' Rory pounced on her words, shaking his head, and the smile that had been there faded somewhat, his voice adopting a more serious tone. 'Things don't always have to escalate into a crisis to justify you being concerned.'

'I know,' Eleanor admitted, but as Rory continued talking her face dropped, listening to the raw anguish behind his words, wishing she had the courage to put her hand out and reach for him.

'My brother died from an asthma attack, sitting on a children's ward, undoubtedly with doctors and nurses around him. I was only eight at the time, so I can't say for sure, but from the little I do know, the little pieces I've picked up over the years, there was no one on duty like you. No one who had the courage to pick up the phone and get more help, no one who had the foresight to realise things were getting out of control and more experienced hands were needed.'

Aghast eyes met his, but it wasn't sympathy he wanted so she held her words back, just listened carefully as he continued to speak.

'Eleanor, what if you'd asked Mary if you could call me and she'd said no, that everything was fine?'

She stared back at him, bemused, trying to picture a different scenario, her forehead creasing into a frown as Rory went on.

'Because one day soon it will happen, Eleanor. Maybe not with Mary, because I trust her judgement more than anyone else I know, but one day or night in the not too distant future, you'll be working with a doctor or nurse and you'll know, just know that more experience is required, know that, despite what they say, things aren't under control.

'Call me,' he said firmly. 'And if it makes things easier for you, you don't have to announce it to anyone, just slip off and ask Switchboard to page me. You've no idea how many times I just *happen* to be passing by and drop in.'

A tired smile inched across his lips as the penny dropped.

'So if I'm ever making a real hash of things and you appear over my shoulder dressed in a dinner suit, I know that someone's dobbed me in.'

'I'd probably phrase things a little differently.' Rory smiled. 'But, basically, yes. You did a good job tonight.'

Eleanor nodded, knowing he was winding things up, knowing he was about to move on, to get on with whatever life Rory led when he wasn't around the hospital. All she knew was that she didn't want him to go, didn't want this slice of time standing in the brightly lit forecourt of the ambulance bay, glimpsing insights into a man she was starting to adore, to end.

'I'm sorry.' As he turned to leave her jumbled words halted him. 'I mean, I'm not sorry I called you, I'm sorry for ruining your evening.'

'It isn't ruined. I should make it in time for dessert.' He nodded to the chocolate bar melting in her hand. 'I'm a chocoholic, like you.'

'Still,' Eleanor fumbled, utterly unable to meet his eyes as she threw in a rod and attempted to fish, 'you deserve a night off. It can't be fun, having the hospital keep ringing. I mean, your girlfriend didn't sound too pleased when I rang. She must be sick of us continually dragging you away.'

There was the longest pause.

The longest, and just when Eleanor thought her lungs would burst, just when she thought she would surely explode if he didn't answer, she felt a tug on her line, but it was Rory reeling her in as slowly, slowly she looked up.

'It was my sister you spoke to,' he said, very casually, but a muscle was pounding in his cheek, his eyes holding hers as he very deliberately made things clear. 'We're at a restaurant nearby. It's her fortieth birthday celebration tonight.'

'That's nice.' Eleanor swallowed hard. 'A family do, then?'

'A few close friends as well. Just a small do, you know.'

'Not really,' Eleanor admitted. 'There's no such thing as a small do in my family. My cousin Gina's having her twenty-first in a couple of weeks and she's invited a cast of thousands…' Her voice trailed off, the nervous tirade ending, and for all the world she could have sworn there was something else coming, something he had wanted to say. But she sensed a change in him, the small world they had created dissolving in an instant, ambulance personnel appearing, cars hooting, as if the stage curtain had lifted, plunging them back into their appropriate roles.

'I'd better get back, then.' He smiled, brusquely turning on his heel and calling over his shoulder. 'Goodnight, Eleanor.'

'Goodnight, Rory.'

Come.

Gripping the steering-wheel, Rory's head tightened in horror as he surveyed his near miss with two minutes' worth of hindsight.

The simple word had been on the tip of his tongue.

He'd been about to ask Eleanor to join him, to come along, have something to eat and say hi. And she'd have come, would have walked into the room and charmed everyone—Rory knew that without a doubt. Could picture it in his mind's eye as clearly as if it had happened.

Feel the pats on his back, the quiet smiles and tiny winks, the unspoken question hanging in the air.

Why not?

Why wouldn't he go for the prettiest, sweetest, youngest nurse?

Who would believe or care that none of that had anything to do with it?

Turning on the ignition he let out a ragged sigh, correcting himself with an honest awareness.

The sweetest part had a lot to do with it.

Eleanor Lewis was the sweetest woman he had ever met.

CHAPTER SIX

SHE worried about him.

And for a twenty-three-year-old it was quite a revelation.

Twenty-three-year-olds worried about the interminable gap between pay days, the abundance of shoe shops the city offered, the appalling lack of unattached men. Twenty-three-year-olds weren't supposed to get a knot of anxiety in their stomachs when they came on duty at seven a.m. and the consultant was already there.

Had probably been there since midnight with twelve hours still ahead of him.

And it shouldn't have even entered Eleanor's head to be concerned when he peeled the wrapper off yet another canteen sandwich or fiddled in his pocket for a couple of dollars for yet another can of cola.

But as the weeks slipped by, over and over she worried just how much Rory was taking on, over and over she looked at his impossible workload and the demands the emergency department placed on those wide, strong shoulders. And, not quite so nobly, Eleanor worried over and over if Rory would ever follow up on his casual but very definite suggestion of taking her out again.

It wasn't as if she hadn't given him an opening. Too many times she'd lingered on her way past the ambulance bay, praying for his footsteps to approach her again; too many times she'd looked up expectantly from her magazine in the staffroom when Rory had wandered in and flicked on the television.

All to no avail.

He hadn't meant it.

Over and over Eleanor punished herself with the obvious truth, over and over she told herself she was reading far too much into things—that Rory's casual invitation to do it all again had merely been a polite response to a pleasant evening, that the burning awareness she'd felt that night in the ambulance bay had been one-sided.

But even with both feet nailed to the ground, none of her theories managed to explain away the tension that simmered in the air whenever they were together. That slow, lazy smile she would swear was just for her.

'You look tired.' Mary was as painfully direct as ever, but a few weeks into her role, Eleanor had learnt how to deal with Mary's rather personal observations.

'You're not supposed to say that, Mary,' Eleanor responded, her elbows propped on the nurses' station, chin in her hands as her senior scribbled on the whiteboard, both women enjoying the lull in proceedings before Friday afternoon finally kicked in. 'You're supposed to say that I look amazing, that I look utterly refreshed and ready to face the world.'

'But you don't,' Mary replied, not even bothering to look up. 'You look worn out, in fact.'

'Ah, but come next week,' Eleanor said, smiling at Rory who looked up from the notes he was writing, 'you'll be eating your words. Once everything is in place I'm going to be the most serene person in this department. In fact, come Monday morning you'll all be asking me for my secret.' Pausing for effect, Eleanor awaited a prompt, but when none was forthcoming, when Rory just shrugged and carried on with his notes, when Mary put her glasses back on and carried on updating the whiteboard, Eleanor elaborated further. 'I've bought new furniture.' When no one responded, her voice became louder. 'Lots of it. In fact, I've completely de-cluttered my life. I've thrown out all the rubbish that I dragged from the country and I'm replacing it with streamlined furniture that has heaps of storage space.'

'You didn't pay for delivery, did you?' Mary swung round, aghast. 'What would you go and do a thing like that for when I've got four strapping lads at home?'

A smile wobbled on Eleanor's lips as she met Rory's eyes, smothering a giggle as she carried on talking.

'It comes in flat packs,' Eleanor explained patiently. 'And the taxi driver very nicely helped me get them into the lift.'

'I bet he did,' Rory mumbled, but Eleanor chose to ignore that little gem.

'The reason I might *look* tired is because I've spent the last couple of nights becoming better acquainted with an Allen key.'

'Is that why you've got sticky plasters on every finger?' Rory asked dryly.

'You might laugh now,' Eleanor responded, 'but you won't be laughing next week when I swing into work half an hour early, when I'm putting my hand up for double shifts while smiling serenely at the drunks. It's going to be worth every last cent—out with the old and in with the new. My feng shui must be going through the roof…'

'Your credit-card bill, too,' Mary added dryly, but Eleanor shook her head.

'The bank finally chose to acknowledge my existence and credit my funds from my old branch, so I'm finally in the black.'

'Glad to hear it,' Mary said, ambling off to a cubicle, nodding at a paramedic wheeling in a patient.

Finally alone with Rory, Eleanor bit the bullet, managed to beat back a blush, sound nonchalant even as she delivered the hardest, most practised, sentence of her life. 'We should go to that noodle bar again,' she said lightly, just as she had umpteen times to the bathroom mirror. 'My treat this time.'

She never quite knew how it happened, how the uppermost thing in her mind just flew out of the window in an instant, how idle chatter at the nurses' station and asking the consultant out for a date merely faded into oblivion as her startled eyes darted to the entrance, but something alerted her.

An urgency, a feeling, an instinct that could never reasonably be explained.

An awful sense of foreboding, followed by screams or footsteps—no matter how many times she went over it, Eleanor could never recall which came first as their eyes locked, whether Rory stood or she ran, but suddenly a woman was running towards her. One look at the baby she held in her arms and Eleanor knew life would never be the same again for her; one look at the lifeless, mottled bundle the woman thrust into Eleanor's arms and she knew that her innocence was gone for ever.

This was the very essence of Emergency—a quiet

afternoon turning into mayhem at a second's notice, a race to save a life as the clock ticked mercilessly on.

This was the real world of Emergency nursing— and one Eleanor wasn't sure she wanted to witness.

The world seemed to be moving in slow motion, pausing, freeze-framing in her mind every now and then as they sprang into action... Rory running toward Resus, Mary's grim face as she pulled back the curtain, the poor mother collapsing on the floor, Vicki rushing to help her as Eleanor ran.

Ran with this precious life, remembering somehow that he needed oxygen, registering for a nanosecond that, though all this baby wore was a nappy, though nothing in his clothing told her he was male, the little blank face, that beautiful innocent face that stared blankly as she held him, was the face of a little boy. And somehow she did it, somehow she exhaled her own air into his lungs, holding back the surge of adrenaline and remembering not to breathe out too hard, pummelling that tiny muscular chest with two fingers as she sped along the polished floor, the loud-speaker springing into life as she laid him down on the Resus bed, Mary shouting her orders over the loudspeaker as it screamed out its awful message.

Alerted the rest of the hospital to what Eleanor already knew.

Paediatric arrest in Emergency.

Paediatric arrest in Emergency, resuscitation room.

'Keep up the massage, Eleanor.' Rory was bagging the babe now, pushing oxygen into his lungs with one hand as he pulled equipment from the shelf with the other to intubate him, tubes and airways he didn't need falling onto the floor and kicked away with an impatient foot. 'Mary, get the red dots on him and let's see what we've got.'

But as Rory held up his hand, as Eleanor stopped massaging the tiny chest, it didn't take a degree in nursing to know that the flat line wasn't the picture they wanted to see.

Vicki burst in, talking in rapid shorthand as they worked on. 'Mum fed him, put him down for his sleep at two. She went in half an hour later to check him and found him blue. She insists that he had a pulse when she picked him up, she's a nurse...'

'She started BLS straight away?'

'Yes.' Vicki's voice trembled for a second as her eyes were pulled to the babe. 'She screamed for the father and they drove straight here, they're no more than two minutes away, mum kept up the basic life support the whole time.'

'What's his name?'

'Declan.'

'OK, what's Declan's temp?' Rory asked as Mary put the probe in the small ear.

'It's thirty-six, Rory, he's still warm.' Mary's voice was filled with emotion as she implored Rory to go on.

And he *was* warm. Eleanor could feel the soft warm skin beneath her fingers, could scarcely believe that this beautiful chubby babe could be lying so life-less as she worked on...

'His pupils fixed and dilated.' Rory's voice was grim as he flashed a torch into his eyes, but Mary was having none of it.

'I've got a line into him, Rory.'

There was the tiniest pause, a flicker of hesitation in Rory's knowing eyes.

'We need to be able to tell the parents we did everything.' There was a note of urgency in Mary's voice, a tiny wobble in her hand as she pulled up the meds. 'Rory, we need to be able to go into that room afterwards and look her in the eye and tell her that we did everything we could. The mum said he had a pulse when she found him!'

'OK.' Rory nodded. 'Keep up the massage, adrenaline…'

'Here.' The drug was passed to him before he had even finished speaking. The Resus doors sprang open as the team started to burst in, the paediatric registrar taking over the massage, kneeling up on the bed beside the infant, clearly ready for a long haul. The anaesthetist was watching, helping to suction him as Rory carried on the intubation then taking over the airway once it was secured as Rory continued to call the shots. And through it all, Eleanor felt as if she might vomit, vomit right there in front of everyone. Now she had stopped giving the massage, wasn't running on autopilot but catching up with reality, her breath was coming so fast she was scarcely able to catch it. Wringing her shaking hands together helplessly as the team worked on. Mary the fiercest of them all, snapping orders at her staff with her mouth while listening to the doctors with her ears, every request for medication, every call for equipment met in the briefest of seconds.

And if it hadn't been so awful, if it hadn't been so tragic, Mary would have been an inspiration to watch.

But when forty minutes had passed, forty, long, anguished minutes with no flicker of response in the

tiny little soul that lay there, when every drug on the
trolley had been used, when every last chance had
been given, it was Rory who sadly but firmly ended
it.

Rory held his stethoscope to the babe's chest, his
eyes on the monitor, his jaw set firmly as for the
longest time he stared, the benefit of doubt long since
gone, the paediatrician sitting wearily back on his
heels, the bleeps from the cardiac monitor, without
the massage, painfully silent.

'We need to bring the parents in.' Rory's voice was
deep and firm, his eyes moving away from the monitor. 'There's been no response since the baby came
into the department. We're not going to get him
back.'

Eleanor's pleading eyes met his then, held them,
so filled with tears she could barely focus, but Rory
carried on talking, answering the question that buzzed
in her mind. 'If, and I don't believe we would, but if
somehow we did get him back, did get his heart to
start beating again, it would only be to take him to
Intensive Care to die there. There's nothing, *nothing*
more that we can do except be there for the parents.
If everyone's agreed, we'll bring them in now.'

He eyed the room, stared at the baby, the awful air
of resignation that filled the room stifling Eleanor now
as she shook her head, watched as Rory's huge hand
stroked the tiny pale cheek, a sob escaping her lips,
the brimming tears cascading unchecked down her
cheeks as she realised it was really over. Nothing they
could do, nothing modern medicine could offer,
would bring Declan back. Blindly shaking her head
at the horror of it all, Eleanor knew she couldn't
watch, couldn't watch those poor, poor parents com-

ing in, couldn't look on a moment longer. And whether or not it was the right thing to do, whether Mary would scold her later, at that moment in time Eleanor truly didn't care. Turning on her heel, she frantically fumbled to open the sliding doors, determined to escape, to get out of the resuscitation room before she completely broke down.

'Sister Lewis!' She could hear Mary calling her, once, twice, but she ignored it, running along the side corridor, holding the sobs in her bursting lungs, pushing open the changing-room doors and sinking onto the bench, wretched sobs racking her body, hating a world that could take away something so precious, hating a world that could be so cruel. If this was Emergency, if this was what was expected of her, to watch, to partake in the end of a tiny life, then she simply couldn't do it.

Simply wasn't up to a job that could rip out her heart and throw it across the room.

How long she sat there she wasn't sure, but the sobs had receded when the door pushed open, a sodden handkerchief in her hand as she reached the gulping stage, not even looking up as Mary walked in.

'Sister Lewis. Eleanor.' Mary's voice was firm but kind, and she made her way in unacknowledged, sitting beside her on the tiny bench as Eleanor stared down at her hands.

'The loss of a baby is, without a doubt, the hardest part of this job, and I'm only very sorry that you had to witness it so early in your career.

'Vicki's still reeling,' Mary carried on gently. 'She's crying in the staffroom now. It touches us all, Eleanor.' Mary's voice wavered. 'You can think you're prepared, go to all the lectures, read all the books, but nothing, nothing can prepare a person for what we witnessed today. You'll remember this for ever.'

Eleanor nodded. 'I couldn't stay. I just couldn't bear to see the parents.'

'You stayed while you were needed,' Mary said softly, the telling off Eleanor had anticipated clearly not about to ensue. 'And you were wonderful, Eleanor. You started massage as soon as the babe was in your arms; you did everything that I would have done. Normally, I'd have asked Vicki to take over, I don't take chances with little ones, I wasn't going to let this be a practice run for you. But you were doing so well, there wasn't any need to have someone else step in.'

'Not well enough, though.' Tears were still rolling down her cheeks, but silent ones now, her head occasionally shaking as images of all she had witnessed trickled in.

'As Rory said, there was nothing any of us could have done. He was dead when he came in. I probably pushed too hard for Rory to carry on the resuscitation.'

'The mum said he had a pulse.'

'Maybe he did for a while,' Mary said knowingly, 'and maybe mum wanted to believe she could feel one. Rory was right, there was nothing to be done.'

Eleanor nodded, chewing on her red swollen lips, her eyes finally turning to her senior.

'I can't do it, Mary. I can't go back out there. If this is what it's about then I don't think I want to be a part of it. Maybe I should go and work on the wards…'

'You'd be wasted,' Mary retorted swiftly. 'And

that's said with no discourtesy to the work the nurses do on the wards. But you're an Emergency nurse, Eleanor, that's all you want to be—you told me so at your interview.' Mary stared back at her, her expression not so soft now and her voice firm as she stood up. 'Tania, that's the mother, she wants to hold her baby now. She's in the interview room. I've taken all the equipment off Declan and I've cleaned him up. Now, what I want you to do is to wrap Declan in a shawl and take him to his mother.'

'No!' Her response was instant, Eleanor's head shaking firmly as Mary headed for the door. 'You can't make me do it, Mary. You can sack me if you want, you can have my notice tomorrow, but I can't face the mother…'

'One day you'll be in charge, Eleanor.' Mary's voice was so definite, so absolutely sure that it stopped Eleanor's emotional tirade for a moment. 'Why do you think I tell you off all the time? Why do you think I'm constantly on your back? Why do you think I've made you work alongside me for three months? It isn't for the good of my health, Eleanor— that I can assure you. It's because you've all the makings of a grand emergency nurse and hopefully you'll be around long after I'm gone from here. Hopefully a bit of me will rub onto you. And one day, in the not too distant future, you might be the nurse in charge, you could be the one dealing from start to finish when a baby is brought in, and if you don't go out there and face Tania then you might just as well empty your locker out now. As hard as this is for us, it doesn't compare to the grief that woman's feeling, and hiding in a changing room isn't going to help anyone.'

She let her words sink in for a moment.

'You know what I'm saying is right, and that's why you are going to wash your face, that's why you are going to take that baby back where he belongs. With his mother.'

'What will I say to her?'

'Nothing.' Mary shrugged but it wasn't dismissive. 'Something. I don't know, Eleanor. You'll have to work that one out when you see her. But Tania handed Declan to you when she came into this department and you should be the one to hand him back to his mother, yes, with a heavy heart, but with the comfort of knowing that everything possible was done.'

She left her alone then, but not for long. Just long enough for Eleanor to wash her face and blow her nose and do the hardest nursing task she could ever have imagined.

Rory was in there, looking every one of his thirty-five years. Lines she had never even seen before seemed grooved on his face as he looked up at her arrival. The chaplain was in there, too, standing up as she knocked quietly and pushed the interview-room door open, walked in with the tiny wrapped bundle.

And she expected wails, shuddering grief to unleash as she stepped inside, but there was a quiet dignity in the room, a proud but painful air of acceptance as Tania held out her arms and took the precious bundle from Eleanor, her eyes not moving from her babe. Eleanor stood for a solemn moment as Tania's cheek met her son's.

'I'm so sorry for your loss.'

It was all she could say, all she could possibly say in the face of such grief, and Rory met her eyes, nodded his quiet thanks as she turned for the door, slipping quietly outside, eternally grateful that Mary was waiting there for her.

'Good lass.' Were tears in those smiling Irish eyes? Eleanor was sure there were. 'Now, let's get on with looking after the living.'

CHAPTER SEVEN

It was long, long after their shift should have ended when Eleanor finally pulled out her hair tie and shook her long hair free and Mary pulled off the stethoscope that constantly hung, along with her glasses, around her neck. But no one was complaining, no one was claiming overtime today. As Mary patiently explained, continuity of care was vital in cases such as these. Too many faces would prove way too confusing for the parents at this awful fragile time.

And the care had gone on long after Declan had died. Eleanor ringing the SIDS—sudden infant death syndrome—support group, who sent out a volunteer to be with the parents and guide them through the fog of grief that engulfed them now. Rory contacted the family GP and the coroner, prescribing medication to stop Tania's milk, endlessly sitting with the parents, answering their questions as best he could until finally they had done all they could. Finally it was time for this awful shift to end.

'How are you doing?' It was the first time he had really spoken to her, the first time they had been alone since Declan had first arrived.

'OK.' She gave a stiff nod, shutting him out, but still he pushed on.

'Do you understand why I ended it?'

'I do.' Eleanor held up her hand, not really ready to go over it just yet, and Rory seemed to understand.

'Well, if you think of anything, if there's anything

you need to know, you just have to ask. I'm here if you need to talk.'

'What about you?' Her eyes turned to him then, unwittingly perhaps, but as soon as the words were out she realised she'd hit a nerve.

'I'm OK.'

'I'll never be OK with it.' She stared back at him, honesty blazing in her red-rimmed eyes. 'I don't care how experienced I get, how used to Emergency I become, I swear, Rory, that I'll never be OK with what happened today.'

'Are you ready, Rory?'

Mary was back. The nursing sister gone now, dressed in a pale blue dress and sensible shoes, her handbag firmly over her shoulder.

'Five minutes.' Rory looked up from his notes, pulling fifty-dollar notes out of his wallet and handing them to Mary. 'Pier and Vicki went on ahead, but no doubt the kitty's a bit depleted by now. You can start getting them in and I'll join you.' Handing Mary the money, he held it in her hand for a second too long. 'Are you all right, Mary?'

'I will be when I'm out of here. Come on, then, Eleanor,' Mary said crisply. 'I think I've earned my port and lemon.'

'Sorry?' Eleanor stared at the two of them, nonplussed.

'Have you not worked an early shift on a Friday yet, Eleanor?'

'No.' Eleanor shook her head. 'I've been on nights, lates, days off,' she answered, Mary practically dragging her by the arm now. 'Where are we going?'

'To the pub.'

Shaking Mary off, her shocked eyes turned to Rory.

'To the pub, after what just happened?'

'We always go to the pub on a Friday.' Rory put down his pen, meeting her face on. 'Whoever the consultant or registrar on is, he takes the early staff to the pub on a Friday. It's tradition.'

'No.' It came out too sharply and Eleanor fought to keep her voice even. 'Look, you lot go—I'm just not up to it. I'd really rather go home.'

'To do what?' Rory asked perceptively. 'Cry your heart out again?'

'Probably,' Eleanor admitted, 'but even if I go to the pub I'll only be delaying the inevitable. Look, I understand that it's tradition and everything, but I'm really going to have to give it a miss.'

'Why?'

Why couldn't he just let it go? She didn't answer, just stared helplessly back at him, but Rory must have read her mind.

'Because it seems wrong to go out socialising when a baby has just died?' When Eleanor nodded hesitantly, he continued talking. 'As callous as it seems, as wrong as it might first appear, it's the right thing to do, Eleanor. I'm exhausted, no doubt Mary and Vicki and the rest of the team are, too, undoubtedly there's a million reasons why we should all just call it a night and head straight for home. But we're a team,' he said softly. 'A team that, whatever darkens these doors, leans on each other, lets off steam with each other, and now and then, especially on a Friday, we're a team that socialises with each other. If we didn't go out whenever something tragic happened, the Friday night tradition would have ended years ago.

'You need friends around you in this job,' he finished softly, 'if you're going to survive.'

And friends they were.

Even Pier seemed to have been temporarily promoted from agency nurse to part of the team, holding a glass of Chardonnay in one hand and waving frantically with the other when finally Eleanor and Mary appeared. And though work wasn't mentioned, though it was clearly out of bounds, the sympathetic smiles that greeted them, the gentle pats on the back as they moved over and made room, spoke volumes.

'Here you are, Mary.' Vicki pushed a port and lemon over and Mary took a rather prim sip. 'What's your poison, Eleanor?'

'A cola, thanks.' Eleanor managed a watery smile. The last thing she needed was alcohol right now. If her guard was lowered even an inch the tears would start again, but Vicki was having none of it, disappearing to the bar and returning with a glass of wine. 'They'd already opened a bottle, for Pier.' She grinned, rolling her eyes as Pier sipped daintily.

And they were wonderful.

Every last one of them, chattering on yet including Eleanor every step of the way, scolding Mary when she rummaged in her bag and produced the biggest slab of hazelnut chocolate Eleanor had ever seen and cracking it open on the table.

'They're going to bar you, Mary.' Rory had arrived, and Eleanor felt her heart do a flip. His tie was still on but loosened, his hair a bit tousled, but he still was easily the most commanding presence in the bar. 'How many times have they told you that you're only supposed to eat what you purchase here?'

'And I've told them that when they start selling chocolate, I'll start buying it, but till then…' she popped a piece in her mouth '…I'll bring my own. Anyway, as if they'd bar us. We're their best customers.'

They certainly drank enough!

Eleanor nursed her glass of wine as the party got louder. Rory also held back, sticking to a couple of beers while the rest of the Emergency mob knocked it back at an alarming rate. Maybe that's how they survive it, Eleanor mused, when finally the day caught up with her, when finally she couldn't paint on a smile a moment longer. Maybe in a couple of years she'd be swilling it down with the rest of them, blotting out the horrors she'd seen, but right here, right now all she wanted to do was go home.

'That's it for me.' Putting a hand over her glass as Pier tried to top her up, she smiled at the crowd around the table. 'I really ought to go.'

She expected some sort of protest, but thankfully her brief appearance had, it would seem, been enough.

'Me, too.'

Swallowing hard, her cheeks darkened as Rory stood up, shaking his head as a jug of beer was pushed towards him. 'Better not. I'm on call this weekend—I think an early night is called for.' Pulling on his jacket, he smiled at all his staff.

'Thanks for all your hard work this week, guys. You were great as always.'

They stepped out onto the street together, Eleanor blinking as the late evening sun's glare momentarily blinded her. And as the world came into focus—never had Melbourne looked more beautiful, the street lined with elms as green as the trams that clattered along the middle of streets lined with tables and chairs, the whole town, it seemed, taking advantage of the gorgeous bosky weather—she stood a moment, her eyes lingering on a couple pushing their baby in its pram. And as beautiful as it was, as perfect as the scene might be, Eleanor knew it wasn't really so.

'Hard to imagine, isn't it?' Again Rory had read her mind. 'Hard to imagine that the world just carries right on.'

'Do you ever get used to it?'

Rory shook his head. 'You learn to deal with it, I guess, but you never get used to it. The day I do is the day I resign.'

Eleanor gave a low laugh. 'I tried to today,' she admitted, and Rory nodded.

'Mary said.'

'Oh, I bet she did.' Eleanor gave a rather undignified snort. 'I bet she also told you how she found me bawling my eyes out in the changing room. Nothing changes, does it? I mean, Mary just never knows when to be quiet.'

'Don't be too harsh on her.' He stared at her, as if debating whether to continue. 'She wasn't gossiping. I called her into my office for a chat.'

'An off-the-record one?' Eleanor grinned but her smile faded as Rory gave a sad nod. 'She felt bad about what she'd done to you…'

'To me?' Eleanor shook her head, bewildered. 'But she was brilliant with me. If it wasn't for Mary I'd be clearing out my locker now.'

'Mary lost a daughter to SIDS or cot death, as it was known then.' As her hands flew to her lips he carried on talking. 'I'm not telling tales out of school.

Everyone knows about it, now and then she talks about it, and no doubt she'll tell you herself soon. She didn't want to go to the parents, Eleanor,' he explained. 'She simply couldn't do it, but in turn she felt awful that she'd forced you to do what she wouldn't do herself.'

'Of course she didn't want to,' Eleanor whispered. 'Of course she was right to send me…'

'That's what I told her,' Rory agreed. 'And I also told her that, as selfish as she thought she was being, if she hadn't thought you were up for the job she'd have done it herself, whatever the emotional cost. She thinks a lot of you, you know.'

Eleanor nodded slowly. 'I think a lot of her, too.'

'Everyone has their Achilles' heel, Eleanor. Even the toughest, fiercest, most dismissive of us has a soft spot. Sometimes you have to read between the lines a bit.

'I'm glad you changed your mind, by the way. Glad you didn't end up resigning.'

'I'm glad, too.' She gave a small eye-roll. 'Well, not glad exactly, but I didn't come all this way to fail. I love Emergency nursing, so if that's what I want to do I suppose I'm going to have to get used to it.' She gave a wry smile. 'Or, as you said, learn to deal with it.'

'You don't have to deal with it on your own, though.' The normally casual comment seemed to take on new meaning, an utterly respectable conversation diving suddenly into uncharted territory.

Sure she must have misheard, sure she must somehow have misinterpreted its meaning, erring on the side of caution, she flashed a casual smile that belied the butterflies dancing in her chest. 'I know.' She nodded. 'Everyone's been great.'

Nothing in his expression changed. Only his eyes, dark navy eyes staring right at her as again he spoke. 'I mean you don't have to be alone tonight.'

'What, more noodles?' Terrified of making a fool of herself, chiding herself for her presumption, she managed a shake of her head. 'I'm really not that hungry.' Glancing down at her watch, Eleanor hoisted her bag higher on her shoulder. 'I'd better go.' She turned, but he stood still and Eleanor knew there and then that the night wasn't over, that nothing he had said had been misinterpreted, that as sure as night followed day, Rory was coming home with her. She turned her head. Those eyes were still watching her, a look she couldn't read on his face, and she understood his trepidation, for she felt it, too, understood the magnitude of what was transpiring as without a word he held out his hand, his fingers closing around hers so strong and warm, so safe and knowing.

Maybe they *were* just drowning their sorrows, maybe they were merely partaking in a rather more intimate ritual than the one going on in the bar, taking solace in a refuge that was only temporary, but as she pushed her front door open, as they entered her tiny flat together, for the first time since she had arrived in Melbourne Eleanor felt as if she was coming home, and the sexual tension that had crackled around since they'd first met rumbled ever louder as they stepped inside. Eleanor knew in a flash that the torturous trip to Ikea, the endless hours assembling furniture had had absolutely nothing to do with rejuvenating her feng shui. Instead it had everything to do with Rory Hunter and this moment that simply had to happen.

'Very nice.' He looked around at the endless shelves she'd built, the smell of paint still in the air despite the open window.

'How long did all this take you to build?'

'Not long,' Eleanor lied.

'Nice views,' Rory mused, glancing out of the window, the trendily tied knots of her new sheer net curtains allowing a delicious glimpse of the glittering Melbourne skyline. 'It's a nice place.'

'Well, it's a bit small.' Eleanor shrugged blithely, even though it was the understatement of the century. If they both exhaled at the same time, their chests would meet. 'But thankfully I'm very tidy.'

'Really?' Rory frowned, watching as she dumped her bag on the sofa and threw her keys onto the coffee-table.

'Obsessively so.' Eleanor smiled, determined that not for a single moment would he think this clean-up might have been in the vague hope he'd take her up on her offer for noodles.

'Do you fancy a glass of wine?'

He followed her into the kitchen, watching with a slightly raised eyebrow as she pulled a bottle from the wine rack and fiddled with a very complicated-looking corkscrew.

'This is very good wine,' he commented, taking over when Eleanor's efforts were clearly going to render them thirsty, burying his smile in the task as Eleanor frantically pulled the price stickers off two matching glasses.

'I like it.' Eleanor smiled brightly, taking the bottle and pouring the heavy full-blooded red into two wine-glasses, taking a sip and wondering what the hell all the fuss was, as it tasted no different to her usual fare. 'Would you like some olives?'

He blinked back at her.

'Or I could put out some nuts.'

'No.' He stared back at her, every muscle in his face concentrating on not laughing—though not at her, never at her. 'No, thank you, the wine's just fine.'

'Shall we go through?'

They never made it to Eleanor's *lounge*. The rumblings that had been building culminated now, exploding like a clap of thunder. Rory carefully took the glass from her trembling hands and laying it on the kitchen bench, eyeing her for one long, exquisitely torturous second as she stood there staring back. His arms moved up, catching the wall either side of her as she stood with her back to it, that delicious mouth finding hers, and for a second not moving, just a murmur, eyes closing simultaneously as skin met skin, the sweet, sweet union of lips finally meeting, savouring the contact, the release of tension that had lingered unacknowledged for so long now. His tongue sliding between her parted lips, his hand cupping her face, kissing her deeply, the rough texture of his chin a sharp contrast to the soft reverence of his kiss. And she kissed him back, slowly at first, revelling in the balmy decadence of his touch until it wasn't enough, until the simmering spark ignited, thundering like a bush fire, flames licking the recesses of her body, quivering inside. His urgency matched Eleanor's now as he pulled at her blouse, ripping until the white buttons pinged onto the floor, staring in awe at her splendid bosom encased in lace. And his hands were there, responding to her unvoiced pleas, pulling back the lace, massaging her swollen nipples, the palm of his hand cupping the soft warm flesh until his tongue, blissfully cool, teasingly flicked them, and though it was divine, delicious even, though his very touch made her dizzy, suddenly it wasn't enough. She needed more, the flickering pulse in her groin more insistent now as his hands slid up her skirt, catching her unawares, her thighs quivering expectantly as she dared to hope for more. So overwhelming was the sensation she truly thought her legs would buckle beneath her.

But then he was holding her.

Scooping her up in his arms, scanning the tiny hallway with hungry eyes, and she would have pointed, would have told him where the bedroom was, but it was so much nicer to go on kissing him, so much nicer to lie in his arms as he carried her to the bedroom, and so utterly appalling to laugh as he laid her on the bed.

'What?' A smile creased his lips as he gazed down. Her tiny hands worked the zipper of his trousers as he yanked off his tie, undoing the first two buttons of his shirt then pulling it off over his head.

'I made this bed.' Eleanor giggled. 'I mean I actually *made* it; I put it together last night. I hope my handiwork's up to it.'

'Time to find out.'

Her laughter strangled in her throat as she saw him for the first time naked, for he was gorgeous, that wide muscular body toned and as utterly gorgeous as Eleanor had secretly imagined. But the bit that mattered, the velvet steel that drew her eyes, catapulted her into mental spasm, was satin in her hands as she drew it closer. And as tiny as she was, he made her feel smaller, dwarfed her with his sheer masculinity, but her giggles started again as she ran a teasing hand along his thigh, the rough stubble of her earlier handiwork a contrast to the soft blond hairs that encased his thighs.

'What happened here, Rory?' she whispered.

'Would you believe me if I told you some nurse shaved me?'

'She didn't.'

Side on, they faced each other, her hands exploring him, tiny gasps escaping her open lips as his hands slid between her legs, parting them assuredly, his finger working a magic she hadn't dared believe in, his palm rhythmically massaging her swollen mound as she held him in her hands, held him as he grew under her touch, guiding him towards her when she knew she couldn't last a second longer, that if he didn't enter her, didn't fill her this very instant, surely she would die. And he knew instinctively what was needed. The flush of colour scorching along her breasts, meeting her cheeks as her lips gasped open, a frenzied, tiny scream as he entered her. Her slender legs coiled around his hips, they moved together, gripping for dear life, her hands clinging on the sheen of his back, so intense the feeling, so utterly, utterly overwhelming, an unsustainable force that must surely, surely end. But he rode her harder, taking her further than she had ever thought possible, her blond hair darkened with a hard-earned sweat. She needed this, needed the oblivion his touch brought, needed to escape from this cruel world to the dizzy height of his love-making. And when she could take it no more, when her most intimate parts throbbed a silent tune he danced it, too, filling her, taking her, possessing her, until, spent utterly, deliciously spent and exhausted, they lay together, holding each other, shutting out the horrors of that day.

Secretly dreading tomorrow.

CHAPTER EIGHT

RORY woke first. The flimsy curtains no barrier against the rising sun, fingers of light creeping across the dishevelled room. Gently he untwined himself, wrapping the sheet around Eleanor's shoulders as she murmured her protest, propping himself up on his shoulder and gazing down on her as she slept.

She looked eighteen.

Vulnerable, fragile and young.

A deep breath stifled a sigh, his eyes dragging the room, taking in the photos, the mum and dad, brothers and sisters, her graduation photo a shelf of memories and achievements that had only just started, a future, a career, a life, glittering before her, and how, he begged of himself, could he take it all away?

Take away the dream she had cherished since childhood.

And he would be taking it away from her.

Rory knew that without a shadow of a doubt. Knew that if he followed his heart, continued what he had started, Eleanor's dreams would have to end.

That the small-minded world of the hospital wasn't quite ready for a blossoming romance between a twenty-three-year-old nurse and a thirty-five-year-old consultant.

If she moved to the wards, though, if they weren't working alongside each other... A tiny surge of hope flickered, but reality instantly doused it.

How could he ask her to give up her dreams?

Cursing himself inside, berating himself for his lack of foresight, he screwed his eyes closed, hating himself for taking this fragile, trusting heart and breaking it.

She saw him then, shoulders hunched, eyes closed, regret etched in every feature, and even though it broke her heart, surprisingly it was easy.

Easy to do the right thing by the man she loved.

'Don't.'

His eyes flicked open as she spoke.

'Don't regret it,' she whispered. 'We needed each other last night, needed to escape, needed…' Her voice trailed off, waiting for him to speak, waiting for him to fill the horrible void, but when silence followed it was Eleanor that filled it, her voice falsely light. She stretched like a cat so she didn't have to look at him.

'Rory, this could never work, we both know that. You know what this would do to us both if this gets out. Just think what it would do my bimbo status if—'

'Don't talk like that,' he broke in fiercely, but Eleanor just shrugged.

'A couple of months here and already I'm in bed with the consultant. Can you imagine the gossip?'

He could. Black, churning bile rose in his throat as he pictured it—the whispers, the winks, the innuendos—and even if he could take it, even if he could get through it, he simply couldn't do it to her.

Couldn't put her through the mill again for an affair that could surely never last.

And it could never last.

Rory knew that deep down.

Not with everything stacked against them before they'd even started.

'Rory.' Her smile wavered only slightly, and the tears that glittered in her eyes could have been from the fierce glare of the early morning sun. 'I'll be OK.'

'You're sure?'

She nodded bravely. 'You'd better go, otherwise someone might see you on their way to work.'

He opened his mouth then closed it, shaking his head before finally speaking. 'I was about to say that I'm sorry, but it would be a lie.'

'I know.' Tears were dangerously close now. 'No regrets?'

'Only this bit.'

Again she nodded, words failing her as he picked up his clothes and dressed.

'Eleanor?' Never had he looked more beautiful, never had he looked more unobtainable…

'Don't.' She said it again, though not quite as firmly. 'Let's just leave it there, shall we?'

Which was easier said than done. The second the front door quietly closed, the second he left her, the tears that had been there since last night surfaced. She clung to the pillow still warm from where he had slept, smelling the tangy scent of him, wishing more than she had ever wished in her life that the gulf that separated them hadn't been quite so insurmountable, that somehow he could have seen her for what she was.

Not a child who wanted him but a woman who needed him.

CHAPTER NINE

ELEANOR dreaded seeing Rory again.

Almost as much as she dreaded not seeing him.

The whole weekend spent staring at the phone, determined not to answer it on the first couple of rings.

But no one rang—well, apart from her mum, a couple of friends back home and Pier ringing to see if she fancied sampling breakfast in St Kilda. But the one person she wanted to hear from remained steadfastly silent.

Even the short walk to work on Monday was fraught with indecision. She was tempted to turn tail and run, to flee to the relative safety of her flat and ring in sick.

Mary's ill-disguised fury was far more appealing than Rory avoiding her eye.

But she was made of sterner stuff than that, Eleanor reminded herself, slamming her bag into her locker and re-tying her hair. He was probably expecting her to phone in sick, Eleanor thought darkly, probably hoping she'd flee back to the country and he'd never have to face her again.

Well, bad luck, Mr Hunter.

She could scarcely believe the venom behind her own thoughts, the beauty of Friday night, the amicable parting on Saturday, distorted now, shattered beyond recognition after two days of tears and two nights alone.

'Right!' Mary was ready for action, clapping her

hands together, revitalised after her weekend off. 'There you are, Eleanor.' Pointedly she glanced at her watch. 'Rory's giving the doctors' lecture in the staffroom. Grab a coffee. If you hurry you'll be there for the start!'

Appalled, Eleanor prayed she'd somehow misunderstood, shaking her head as Mary shooed her away. 'But it's a doctors' lecture,' Eleanor protested. 'They're hardly going to want me there.'

'Nonsense,' Mary said briskly. 'Anyway, the term "doctors' lecture" is a misnomer, it's open house for all the emergency staff. It's called a doctors' lecture because he expects all the interns to be there. You'll learn a lot from listening to him. Rory's very good at passing on his experience.'

An extremely witty response would have been more than merited, but it would have been wasted on Mary, Eleanor consoled herself, taking for ever to make a simple coffee, taking three false starts to finally push open the staffroom door and step nervously inside.

It was small consolation, as every eye turned to the latecomer, that the speaker looked as uncomfortable as her.

'I was just explaining,' Rory addressed her as finally she found a seat, 'that statistically, in the next six months, someone in this room will examine a patient and send them home, sure they are well, only to have them arrive back in the department critically ill or, worse, receive a phone call either from the coroner or a solicitor to say that the patient subsequently died.'

It was a chilling statistic, enough to force Eleanor's

attention, to push her very raw grievances aside and actually focus on the lecture.

'So what can we do?' Rory's eyes worked the room. 'Is there anything we can do to prevent this scenario?'

'Be more thorough.' A rather eager-looking doctor Eleanor hadn't yet worked alongside pushed up his glasses and leant forward. 'Make sure the notes we write up aren't just medically accurate but legally sound.'

'You can try.' Rory shrugged. 'And in theory it sounds good, but you haven't worked a Friday night in this place yet. If we practise medicine merely to appease lawyers, I can guarantee that a week into the experiment someone will die waiting while we're being so *thorough.*

'We could go on for hours.' Rory glanced at his watch. 'But we've only got one. There isn't time to go into examinations, isn't time to throw up scenarios for each and every case that might present itself at our doors. Instead, in this lecture we're going to concentrate on looking at the bigger picture, getting away from the scientific and looking at the human element, see if we can't use what we already know to help us in our diagnoses.'

He held them in the palms of his hands, and with grudging admiration Eleanor listened, amazed she could put the pain of the weekend behind her, could take a sip of coffee that had already gone cold, and listen, really listen to what Rory was saying.

'An eighteen-month-old presents with sudden collapse. The mother's hysterical, but the baby, by the time the mother's driven it here, is pink and well, smiling and laughing. She swears he was pale and lifeless at home, she's got three other children, and till now they've never been really sick. She asks where the waiting room is, disappears to ring her husband and pull him out of work then comes back and asks what's happening. So what is happening, guys? What are you going to do?'

'FBC, U&Es, lumbar puncture—' Dr *Eager* started.

'OK, they've already been done,' Rory broke in, a wry smile on his face. 'Things move fast in this fantasy emergency department. You've even managed to convince the radiographer to rush through chest and abdo films, too. His ears and throat are as clear as a bell and the paediatrician's even been in and had a look. Every test, every examination has come back as normal. Dad's arrived now, wants to take the baby home. The paediatricians are happy to let him go and have passed the buck to you, and frankly you can't find a thing wrong with him.

'On paper he looks good,' Rory said softly. 'On paper everything about this baby tells you to sign him off and send him home with his mum, so why wouldn't you? What could possibly make you want to keep him?' He looked around the room slowly, smiling slightly as everyone avoided his gaze, praying not to be the one he picked on for an answer. Only Eleanor stared back, determined to meet him face on. If ever she was going to show him that her career came first, that Friday night wasn't going to divert her from her chosen path, now was the time.

Now was the time to take a deep breath and, given the amount of grey matter in the room, possibly make a complete fool of herself.

'Instinct.' Eleanor stared right at him as she spoke, her palms moist with sweat as every eye in the room turned towards her. 'A feeling that something isn't quite right?'

'Good.' A small cough was the only indication he wasn't one hundred per cent comfortable. 'Listen to your inner voice. But instinct isn't necessarily going to help you present a valid case to the paediatrician. What we need to do is analyse that instinct, work out why something just doesn't feel right and eloquently present it to our peers. I've given you a lot of information. I want you to think about it for a moment…'

He gave them two moments, in fact, but still the penny didn't drop, nervous eyes frowning at each other as they awaited enlightenment. 'You've heard of the boy who cried wolf?' His voice was louder suddenly, snapping them all to attention. 'The mum who calls an ambulance for an earache. Well, let's look at the reverse for a moment. Here we've got a mother of four, a woman who has never graced the emergency department in her life—'

'We didn't know that,' Dr *Eager* broke in, but Rory shook his head.

'She didn't know where the phone was.' Rory's voice was firm. 'Use every clue the patient gives. You've only got a few minutes to form an opinion, a few minutes to make an evaluation, so you have to use every means available.

'This woman, this experienced mother of four, is telling you her baby is sick, that something happened today that she can't really explain and clearly you can't either.

'Keep him.' Rory stared at each and every one present in turn. 'Ring the registrar, the consultant, tell Paeds to get their backsides down here and admit him. Yes, you might look an idiot, might be proved wrong, but if something doesn't fit, if something just doesn't seem right, a good idea is to step back out of that cubicle, look at what's brought this person here, go over again all the clues you've been given. Whether or not it saves a life, I can guarantee you'll be a better doctor for it. Or nurse,' he added, not quite meeting her eyes.

'He's good, isn't he?' An intern, who could only be a year or so older than Eleanor, turned around and gave her a smile.

'It's very interesting,' Eleanor admitted.

'And so much easier on the ears when the lecturer's simply divine.'

He could have any of them, he could have them all, Eleanor thought to herself darkly. He could flash that winning smile and take his pick of the beauty on offer, and like a fool she had succumbed.

Like a stupid fool she'd tumbled into bed with barely a thought for the consequences, barely a thought of how to survive in a department where she'd slept with the boss.

Rory wound it up as the crowd gradually dispersed, the pretty intern lingering way too long to congratulate him. Eleanor attempted to quietly slip away but he called her back and she stood uncomfortably as he cleaned the whiteboard of his random scribbling, made sure every last straggler had definitely left before finally facing her.

'Great talk.' She dazzled him with her smile. 'You really got everyone thinking.'

'Thank you.' He was frowning, her reaction clearly not what he had expected, his eyes concerned as they held hers.

'I'm glad you came to the lecture this morning.'

He gave a small, uncomfortable smile. 'I know it couldn't have been easy for you.'

'Why wouldn't I come?' Eleanor's brisk response obviously confused him. 'I'm here to learn, Mr Hunter, and, as Mary pointed out this morning when I came on duty, you're an extremely experienced doctor. Why wouldn't a gullible, naïve nurse take the opportunity to sharpen her skills?'

'Eleanor, don't.' He closed his eyes for a fraction of a second and she almost regretted the harshness behind her words, the pain that flickered across his face for a second or two almost convincing. 'I'm sorry if I hurt you.'

'But you didn't!' Wide blue eyes blinked back at him. 'Contrary to what you clearly believe, it really wasn't that big a deal.'

'I just wanted to check that you were OK, wanted to be sure…'

'That I'd survived?' Her smile stayed put. She even managed a wave as Pier, coffee and magazine in hand, wandered into the staffroom. 'Don't overrate yourself, Rory, I'm doing just fine.'

CHAPTER TEN

'WHY is love so cruel, Eleanor?'

Pier's question wasn't exactly helping matters. Furiously writing her notes next to Rory, trying to ignore the scent of his aftershave, the occasional brush of his elbow as he scribbled along beside her, she wished, for once, that Pier would just shut up so she could carry on pointedly ignoring Rory.

And she was very good at ignoring Rory, very good at staring right past him, appearing engrossed in a magazine when he came into the staffroom, even managing to politely talk to him if others were present, but not quite meeting his eye. And, as it turned out, Rory was excellent at reciprocating.

They'd started off nice, of course, apologising every time they accidentally banged into each other, supremely polite at every turn, but as days ticked into weeks, as the initial scorching embarrassment finally faded, Eleanor learnt yet another life lesson.

That love unattended didn't simmer along nicely.

That love unattended didn't always boil over.

That love unattended burnt to a black indelible mess that was hell to get off.

'Why am I working on a Friday night when I should be out dancing?' Pier moaned on. 'Dancing with the man I love.'

A reluctant smile wobbled on her lips as she felt more than heard Rory's intake of breath as a mental picture of Pier, dancing, transpired.

'I will tell you why I am not out dancing,' Pier
continued to his reluctant audience. 'Because Gary
has expensive taste, that's why! Tomorrow night he
wants to go to some nice Italian restaurant he has
heard about, tomorrow night he wants to go to a very
exclusive club, so tonight I have to work to pay for
it.'

'Hasn't Gary heard of going Dutch?' Eleanor
asked, without looking up.

'He's Australian,' Pier responded.

'Well, that explains it.'

'Why can't I meet someone straightforward?' Pier
pouted. 'Why do I always end up feeling used?'

'Because you *are* being used.' Eleanor flashed a
very sweet smile. 'Learn from it, Pier, and move on.'

'I don't want to move on,' Pier said. 'I like Gary.'
He gave her an accusing stare. 'I bet you like to be
wined and dined, I bet you wouldn't turn your nose
up at an expensive Italian restaurant and an exclusive
nightclub, I bet you—'

'On the contrary.' Signing her name, Eleanor
snapped the file of papers between the arms of the
staple gun, ramming it down hard with the back of
her hand as she shot Rory a venomous look. 'In fact,
I'm a very easy date. Forget the expensive restaurants,
forget the intimate nightclubs. A glass of Chardonnay
and a bowl of noodles and you're home and dry with
me.'

'Eleanor?' Rory's voice wasn't exactly engaging.
'When you've finished sorting out Pier's love life, or
lack of it, can you give out some Ventolin and
Serotide to Mrs Browne in cubicle four and make sure
she understands about the reducing dose of steroid
medication I've prescribed for her son?' He handed

her the casualty card he had finished writing without even bothering to look up. 'William Browne, four years old with newly diagnosed asthma. I've given the mum the X-rays and she's to go to her own GP tomorrow to get him reviewed.'

'Well, since you put it so nicely.' Eleanor took the proffered card and flashed a false smile. 'How could I refuse?'

It should have been straightforward but, popping her head in to the cubicle, Eleanor knew at a glance it wasn't going to be. Clipping the card to the door, she stepped inside, picking up a box of tissues and wrapping an arm around a sobbing Mrs Browne and guiding her to a chair.

'I'm being silly,' Mrs Browne gulped, accepting the tissues and smiling bravely at her little boy scribbling in a colouring book as he sat happily on the trolley. 'I mean, I know loads of kids get asthma, I know it's a bad time of year for it, it's just I'm so scared.'

'It is scary,' Eleanor agreed. 'You brought William in with what you thought was a chest infection and suddenly you're armed with puffers and peak-flow meters and reducing doses of steroids.' Eleanor gave a sympathetic smile but her voice was reassuring. 'But before you know it you'll be used to it, and William will be, too. It will just take a while.'

'But what if he gets worse? What if he has an attack? I don't know how I'd cope—'

'You'd cope,' Eleanor broke in. 'Did Mr Hunter explain about watching William's peak flow? How they generally tail off before an attack?'

'He did.' Mrs Browne sniffed. 'But he said my GP would go into everything, that William would be fine tonight. He said it was only a mild wheeze he had now and he seemed so busy I didn't like to keep asking stupid questions.'

'They're not stupid.' Standing, Eleanor patted the woman's shoulder. 'I'll ask Mr Hunter to come in and have another word.'

She was sure he would.

Despite the animosity, despite the prickling tension between them, patients had always come first, their differences pushed aside in the name of patient care. But when Eleanor pushed the card back to him and asked him to come and talk to Mrs Browne again, she was stunned by his indifference, stunned that the doctor she still respected could give an irritated shrug when she asked him to go back in to Mrs Browne and reiterate William's care.

'I've already explained it to her.' Picking up the phone, he punched in a few numbers. 'The GP's the person to follow it up—he's the one who should have seen him in the first place. William has mild asthma. The pollen count's through the roof at the moment. In a couple of days he'll be fine.'

'But she doesn't know that,' Eleanor said through gritted teeth. 'She thinks he's about to drop dead at any moment. Oh, come on, Rory, the woman's upset. Will you talk to her again or not?'

'Fine.' Pulling the card from Eleanor's hands, he gave a curt nod. 'After I've sorted out the man in Resus with a pulse rate of thirty and the woman in cubicle two with a black, pulseless foot. Now, can you run a pregnancy test on this patient for me so I can work out if she might be about to collapse due to an ectopic pregnancy?'

She didn't even deign to give him a response.

Of course, for reasons known only to Mary, the pregnancy testing kits were kept under lock and key in the drug room.

'Ignore him,' Mary soothed as Eleanor exploded in fury once they were safely inside the drug room. Her gibbering rage at Rory's callousness demanding an outlet.

'But Mrs Browne was upset! How dare he just dismiss it?' Eleanor responded angrily. 'How dare he trivialise a mother's concerns for her child?'

'He didn't.' Mary explained patiently. 'At least, not to Mrs Browne. He only let off a bit of steam with you, that's what colleagues are for sometimes, Eleanor. Rory *is* busy this morning, and in fairness young William's asthma is probably best dealt with by his own GP. But now that he is here and you've told him how scared the mother is, I can guarantee Rory's in there now, talking to the woman and reassuring her. Sure, no doubt he was hoping she'd take her questions to her GP...'

'But that's so unlike him,' Eleanor moaned, scarcely able to believe it had come to this, that the animosity growing between them might be impinging on patient care. 'Rory's normally the first one to chide us all if we trivialise people's symptoms or say that they're not a "real" emergency—'

'Not with asthma,' Mary broke in, taking a deep breath before she carried on talking. 'Rory hates kids with asthma...'

'But he was great with that little boy, Marcus,' Eleanor refuted, but a small frown was appearing as an uncomfortable memory stirred, the raw anguish in Rory's voice when he had confided in her about his brother, but still nothing added up. Rory had been brilliant with Marcus, she'd seen him in Resus a few times since then, watched in quiet admiration that he could push his own nightmares aside and deal so calmly with an asthmatic patient, given what he had been through. 'He's great in Resus.'

'I'm great in Resus, too.' Mary shrugged. 'At least when a patient's in Resus, you feel as if there's something you can maybe do.' Her voice dropped to a whisper. 'No doubt you've heard by now about my daughter?'

Eleanor nodded, her hands instinctively moving for her senior's arm, holding it for a moment, knowing there was nothing, nothing she could say. Mary acknowledged her touch with a gentle, grateful pat. 'His brother died, you know, had an asthma attack when Rory was just a little boy.' Mary gave a knowing nod. 'I'm telling you this so that you'll watch out for him, the same way Rory watched out for me when that wee angel Declan came in.' Her eyes misted over. 'While there's no better doctor in this building for reassuring a child when they're unwell, when he's talking to the parents, when he's trying to tell them that asthma can be managed, that there's no reason little Johnny can't play football or take up swimming, well, given what he's seen, Rory's always concerned his own fears will come across.'

Eleanor nodded, a deeper understanding descending now, not just for Rory but for Mary and all the staff she worked with. Rory's words rang over and over in her mind.

Everyone has their Achilles' heel, Eleanor. Sometimes you have to read between the lines.

'Now, what are we here for?' Mary asked briskly.

'A pregnancy test,' Eleanor answered, her mind a million miles away, watching as Mary pulled out the keys and fiddled in the cupboard.

Mary thought she had shared a confidence and Eleanor chose not to tell her that she already knew Rory's brother had died, that she knew a little about what made him tick, that for a moment in time Rory had chosen to confide in her.

But not now.

Now he couldn't even tell her he was hurting, would rather feign disinterest than admit the truth.

How had it come to this?

'Here.' Mary broke into her thoughts, thrusting a box of pregnancy test kits at Eleanor. 'And before you ask why I lock them up, it's because if I didn't they wouldn't last five minutes in this place. We'd have every nurse in the hospital running a quick check the minute they were five minutes late. Now, while we're here, why don't we get the pumps for William?'

Eleanor had never stolen anything in her life.

OK, a packet of sweets from the milk bar when she was six, which her mum had made her return, marching her back and standing furiously behind her as she'd stammered out her apology to the owner, swearing she'd never do anything like it again.

So why, then, did her hand pick up two kits as Mary fiddled with asthma meds? Why was her hand slipping one in her pocket, her cheeks a scalding crimson as Mary took back the box with a smile.

She wasn't even late, Eleanor told herself as she stood in the staff loo, staring at a tiny white piece of plastic, minutes ticking away like hours as she awaited her fate. Well, a few days late maybe, Eleanor conceded, but she'd moved home, started a job...

Was pregnant.

Staring at the pale pink cross forming on the blotting paper, Eleanor felt the colour drain from her face. The test had been a quest for reassurance, an end to the nagging question that had been plaguing her for a few days now, sure, so sure that it would put her mind at rest, that she'd be able to toss it in the bin with a rueful smile, move on with her life, put the past where it belonged and learn to live with the pain of rejection.

But now?

Her breathing was coming so fast that for a moment she couldn't catch it, terrified tears filling her eyes as the awful reality started to hit home, berating herself over and over for her own stupidity, anger building inside her as she contemplated Rory's total irresponsibility that night as well.

He should have known better, they *both* should have known better.

They were a doctor and a nurse, for heaven's sake.

A sob escaped her lips as the clichés started taunting her.

A country girl alone in a big city, she could just hear the talk in her home town when she returned with her tail between her legs. And she would return—it was a foregone conclusion.

For how could she possibly stay?

How could she possibly tell him?

Flushing the test down the toilet, she headed for the sink, splashed cool water on her face and briefly caught her own reflection in the mirror, scarcely able to even look herself in the eye.

She'd made the biggest mistake of her life and now she'd have to pay for it for ever.

'I spoke to Mrs Browne for you.' It seemed ironic that Rory was the first person she saw as she came out of the changing rooms. 'I went through everything with her and she's feeling much more confident about taking him home now.'

'Good.' Her throat was so dry she could barely get the single word out, desperate to walk away, to put some space between them, for her shift to end so she could go back to her tiny bedsit and contemplate her appalling future, but for once Rory seemed determined to prolong a conversation with her, his eyes boring into her as she stared somewhere between his shirt collar and shoulder. 'Time management is an essential part of Emergency, Eleanor.' His stern voice was so many light years from the man who had held her, the man who had made love to her, every word, every lie that spilled from his lips only widening the void between them. They both knew the truth, the real reason for his indifference to Mrs Browne. And if he'd rather talk down to her than admit it, couldn't even let her in that tiny bit, then there wasn't a hope for them.

No hope at all.

She shook her head in defeat, a bewildered laugh utterly void of humour escaping her lips as Rory carried on his lecture. 'I'm a consultant, Eleanor, and as much as I'd have liked to spend more time with Mrs Browne, sometimes I have to prioritise. I had very sick patients that needed me, there simply wasn't time to sit down and go over and over all the possible scenarios—that's why I referred her back to her GP.

While I commend your approach to patients, while I
understand that you want to give everyone a hundred
and ten per cent, I have to tell you that it's not always
possible. You have a Pollyanna approach to nursing
at times—'

'Oh, I do, do I?'

He hesitated for a second, as if realising he had
gone too far.

'Eleanor, this was best dealt with by her GP, you
know that as well as I do.'

'Perhaps.' She managed to look at him then, her
chin jutting defiantly, arms folded defensively as her
angry eyes met his. Even if he was her boss, even if
he was the most senior person in the place, at that
moment Eleanor couldn't have cared less. He was the
man who had broken her heart, the man whose child
she was carrying, and if he thought she was about to
stand there and take his rubbish just because she was
a nurse, he had another think coming.

For this afternoon at least, name tags and titles
didn't matter a jot.

'Spare me the lecture, Rory…'

'Eleanor.' His eyes flashed angrily. 'I'm a consultant…'

'So you said.' She flashed a withering smile. 'On
many occasions. And while I respect your position,
Mr Hunter, while I would never do anything to compromise the esteem this department holds you in,
don't you dare stand there and call me Pollyanna.
Don't you dare stand there and feed me a line about
time management and prioritising patients when we
both know…' She swallowed hard, not quite sure
whether to cross the line.

'Both know what, Eleanor?' His voice was stern, his eyes a virtual stranger's, and for Eleanor it was the final straw.

'We both know that you're bleeding inside.'

CHAPTER ELEVEN

ELEANOR had never really understood the stories she'd read about women who'd arrived at hospital in labour, insisting they hadn't known, or women who had given birth in the bath to a baby they hadn't known they'd been carrying.

But now the shoe was on the other foot, she was starting to understand. For if she hadn't done that wretched test, if she hadn't seen the confirmation right there before her eyes, Eleanor could have very easily chosen to ignore her symptoms. Chosen to ignore a bust that was growing like a triffid, chosen to ignore the constant nausea that plagued her.

She tried anyway. Flicking from a TV channel every time a nappy commercial came on, marching past the antenatal clinic on her way to the canteen and absolutely refusing to acknowledge that it might be prudent to make an appointment. But despite her ambiguous feelings about her pregnant status, she didn't take silly risks, duly ducking out when the portable X-ray machine appeared in Resus, making an excuse not to go near when a child came in covered in a chickenpox rash, yet all the time secretly hoping that a magic fairy might wave a wand and make it all just go away.

But even in Eleanor's Pollyanna world, fairies were in short supply.

For Mary, too, it would seem.

'I don't know what to do.' Mary threw down her

139

pencil in exasperation as Eleanor came over. 'I've spent the best part of an hour staring at this off-duty roster and I simply don't know what to do. Can you believe that I'm the only person who's available to work tomorrow afternoon?'

'You're not serious?' Frowning, Eleanor peered over her shoulder at the roster.

'I am,' Mary said. 'It's Vicki's engagement party and half the staff requested the afternoon off. And I've just had two more staff ring in sick this morning, telling me they've got doctors' notes till Monday. I've got people doing double shifts all over the place, but come tomorrow…' Picking up the pencil, she chewed on it for a moment, staring back at the roster. 'You've got that twenty-first birthday party to go to, haven't you?'

Eleanor nodded glumly.

This time tomorrow the entire Lewis family would be descending on the neighbouring town to her home town for a true country party which normally, under any other circumstances, Eleanor would have been looking forward to. A massive white marquee filled with family and friends, catching up with the people she'd missed so much since moving away. Her suitcase was packed in the changing room. As soon as her shift ended she was heading for Spencer Street station and catching the train home, to be met at the other end by her mother.

And Eleanor would have given anything not to go.

She wouldn't even make it off the station platform without breaking down. One look at her mother and the news she wanted to keep a secret would be out in the open.

Nothing got past her mother, nothing at all.

'I'll work.' Eleanor's hand was up in a flash but Mary shook her head.

'You requested this weekend off at your interview, Eleanor. I don't expect you to change your plans, that's not what I was after when I told you my problem.'

'I know that. Honestly, Mary, it's no big deal. Mum will understand.'

She didn't, of course, and Eleanor still had the red ear from the phone call to prove it when she arrived for the shift the following day. But as difficult as the phone call had been, as disappointed as her mother had sounded, for Eleanor the phone call had been a revelation.

'You should be here, Eleanor,' Mrs Lewis had said reproachfully. 'You're a part of this family and you should be there for Gina on her special day.'

'I know that, Mum, but there's nothing I can do.' Crossing the fingers of her free hand, Eleanor had blushed as she'd lied into the phone. 'The sister in charge gave me no choice but to come in. She told me that if I value my job…'

'You should value your family more,' Mrs Lewis scolded before she rang off. 'They're the ones who are always there for you.'

And she was right.

That was why Eleanor's notice was written in her pocket, that's why if a quiet moment eventuated today, she would hand it in to Mary.

Her family would be there for her.

Upset, shocked, disappointed even, but sooner rather than later they'd come around and, like it or not, she needed them. Needed to be surrounded by people she loved during this emotional journey.

Needed the quiet, unwavering support only love could provide.

Rory mightn't be able to give it but she wasn't completely on her own.

'Like our first shift.' Pier nudged Eleanor when handover wrapped up after a few minutes, the department unusually quiet for once. 'You, me and Mary taking on the world.'

'How's Gary?' Eleanor smiled.

'Fabulous!' Pier beamed. 'He's taking *me* out tonight, and I don't care what comes through the doors, come nine p.m. I'm out of here. What about you? Have you got any plans?'

'Not really.' Eleanor shrugged. 'A slushy movie and a slab of chocolate sound about right.'

'Right.' Clapping her hands together, Mary stared at the empty whiteboard. 'Why don't you get on with the stocking up, Pier? You can show the other agency nurses where everything's kept and I'll take Eleanor into cubicle two and do her appraisal. I'll be able to hear if anything big comes in.' In a surprisingly maternal gesture, taking Eleanor by the arm, she gave her a very nice smile. 'This is one appraisal that shouldn't take very long.'

Eleanor took a seat and stared at her knees as Mary started talking.

'As I said to Pier, this won't take long. For once I'm not going to beat around the bush.' Finally Eleanor looked up. 'We're thrilled with your work here, Eleanor. I've spoken to all the senior nurses and doctors and unanimously we agree that you're already a valuable member of the team and we're thrilled to have you on board. I admit, at first I had a few doubts, I thought that after a few weeks the shine might fade a touch, that you couldn't be *that* nice to each and every patient all the time.

'But you are.' Mary stared back at her.

'And watching you work, observing how you treat the patients, has given more than a few of us a wake-up call. Eleanor, it's very easy to be cynical in this game, it's very easy to look at the numbers instead of the people, to see a full waiting room and merely wade through it, but you treat each and every person as if they matter, which of course they do, but sometimes we all need to be reminded of that.

'Now!' Adopting a slightly sterner tone, Mary carried on. 'That said, there are a few areas that can be worked on, a few things I'd like to go through before we look too far ahead. I'd like to give you some more experience in Resus, perhaps send you on a couple of ride-alongs with the paramedics—'

'Mary.' Pulling the envelope out of her pocket, Eleanor held it out. 'I think now might be the right time to give you this.' She stared back at her knees as Mary ripped open the envelope and started to read. 'Before you make any plans for me, I mean...'

'Did you not listen to a word I said?' Mary's face jerked up from the letter. 'You're doing really well, you seemed so happy here. So settled, you even went out and bought all that furniture.'

'I know I did.' Mary's appalled expression wasn't making this any easier. She had expected a murmur of protest perhaps, but Mary seemed genuinely disappointed that she was going, staring at the letter and shaking her head. 'And I have been happy here. I love my work. I've already learnt so much.'

'Then why are you talking about leaving, Eleanor?'

Her voice softened slightly. 'Are you feeling home-sick? Is that what all this is about?'

It wasn't, but it was far easier to nod miserably than to tell the truth.

'I was wrong to let you work this weekend.' Mary patted her knee. 'Take next weekend off, have a long weekend at home with your family and then we'll have a talk. Maybe a small break is all you need.'

'No.' Eleanor shook her head firmly, terrified she might weaken, because as hard as it would be to stay, the thought of leaving was breaking her heart. 'I'm leaving, Mary. If you need me to work over my two weeks' notice then that's fine. I can stay for a month or so till you find someone else.' She gave a wry smile. 'I'm sure I'll be easily replaced.'

'Not necessarily,' Mary murmured, clearly stunned at the turn of events. 'You have all the makings of a grand Emergency nurse.'

'And I still will be,' Eleanor countered, 'but back in the country, back where I belong.'

'What about that manager you didn't like?' Mary's gloves were off now, determined to make her see sense, but Eleanor already had her answer.

'I've grown up in the last few months, Mary. I can deal with Rita with my eyes closed now.'

And she could. Stepping out of the cubicle, she joined Pier, stocking up the trolleys, biting back the tears as she filled the antiseptic bottles and the cotton-wool ball jars. Rita's acid comments were the least of her problems now. Nothing Rita would say could even begin to compare to the gossip that would ignite if she chose to stay.

Mary mightn't realise it, but she was actually doing the department a favour.

Not that she got any thanks.

The letter still in her pocket, Mary returned to the battleaxe Eleanor had first encountered, snapping orders, clearly taking a professional decision way too personally, and by four o'clock Eleanor was tempted to get her bag and go home. If she hurried she could just about make it for the last part of the party, head back to the house with her mum and finally tell her what was really on her mind. But as tempting as it was, as awful as Mary was being, Eleanor couldn't do it. For now at least she was part of the team and her conscience wouldn't quite allow her to leave them in the lurch.

'Paul Lang, in cubicle six.' Mary pushed the card towards her without looking up. 'Can you give him the Buscopan injection Rory just wrote up?'

Eleanor nodded.

'And wear gloves,' Mary added. 'He's a heroin addict.'

'Universal precautions, Mary,' Pier chimed in with a teasing wink. 'We're supposed to take the same precautions with everyone, just because Mr Lang is a heroin addict it doesn't mean he should be treated any differently.'

'I'm not treating him differently,' Mary snarled, clearly not in the mood for humour. 'I'm just pointing out to a young nurse that this patient might be at a higher risk of transferring blood-borne diseases and I'll tell it to the do-gooders if they ask why I'm reminding Eleanor to be extra careful.'

'I'll give the injection. He's a nasty piece of work.' Rory was at the desk now, holding his hand out for the card, but it was a bit late for him to start playing the role of the great protector and Eleanor turned smartly on her heel.

'I'll be fine.'

Swiping her card, she let herself into the drug room, filling a kidney dish with gloves and swabs before pulling out the box for the injection, jumping out of her skin when the door pinged open and Rory appeared, without a word checking the ampoule she held in her hands and watching as she pulled it up with amazingly steady hands.

'Mary said you'd handed in your notice.'

'She didn't waste much time.'

'It's true, then? You're not even going to give it some more thought?'

'I've already given it plenty of thought.' Eleanor bristled.

'I'm sorry you're going.'

He had a nerve. For a second she bit back a smart reply, for a second she stifled the fury that welled inside her, so determined had she been to see this through with a semblance of dignity, but as her eyes snapped to his, as again he lied through his teeth, Eleanor decided to act like the twenty-three-year-old she was, to revel in her immaturity and let him have it.

'No, you're not.' Each word was laced with contempt. 'You're relieved, Rory, bloody relieved that you won't have to face your mistake any more. So don't play games with me, don't you dare stand there and tell me that you're sorry I'm going.'

'I am, Eleanor.' His voice was so convincing she almost believed him. 'I'm sorry that the department is losing a great nurse and, for what it's worth, I'm going to miss you too.'

She let out an incredulous, very undignified snort.

'Mary said that you were homesick, that that was why you were going, but that's not true, is it?'

'At this point I believe I'm supposed to lie, Rory.' She gave him a bitter smile, watching him wince with its delivery. 'I'm supposed to relieve your guilty conscience with a convincing story of how I miss my mum, how the city could never really be home. Well, I'm sorry, but I'm not going to do it. I loved it here, loved this job, and given the chance I'd have done really well. So for all the twenty-three-year-olds that come after me, bear that in mind, will you, when you take them out for a bowl of noodles, when you flash that winning smile and ask for an off-the-record chat.'

'It was never like that.' As she went to open the door he slammed it closed with one hand. 'You know it as well as I do. Look, Eleanor, you leaving completely defeats the purpose. I ended it so you could stay—'

'How very noble.'

'Eleanor, please, will you just listen to me for a moment…?' His voice trailed off as Mary burst in. Because of all that had gone before, she didn't offer a wisecrack, didn't ask what had held them up with a wink and nudge, just nodded to Eleanor to come with her. But as she went to go, Eleanor frowned in angry confusion as Rory picked the conversation up again, for all the world apparently not caring a jot that Mary was now present. 'I want you to think about this.' He glanced at Mary. 'Eleanor's notice is to go no further until I've spoken with her, OK?'

'Fine,' Mary said in a clipped voice, but curiosity was etched on her features as she faked a dismissive shrug. 'Now, can we, please, give Mr Lang his blessed injection and get him out of here?'

Despite Rory's uncomplimentary summing up of the patient, Paul Lang lay quietly as Mary and Eleanor checked his wristband against the card then administered the injection. 'Right, young man,' Mary said crisply. 'Mr Hunter is happy with your ultra-sound and blood work. You're to see your GP if there's any further problems. Eleanor, did you bring the follow-up letter?'

'It's at the desk.' Taking the kidney dish, she disposed of the needle and syringe carefully before picking up the letter and heading back to the cubicle. Paul was already dressed, pulling on some filthy runners and not looking up as Eleanor handed it to him.

'Here,' she offered, but he didn't accept it.

'Don't worry about it,' he mumbled. 'I haven't even got a GP.'

'Well, if you don't feel better, you know where we are,' she offered, but Paul gave a dry laugh. 'I don't think I'm very welcome, do you?' His eyes finally met hers. 'That doctor reckons I'm just putting this stomachache on so I can get some drugs.'

'Not necessarily.' Eleanor gave him a sympathetic smile. 'He investigated you very thoroughly and the injection he ordered is very good for abdominal pain.'

'Whatever you say.' His voice wasn't surly, just resigned, and suddenly Eleanor felt sorry for him, her stance softening as she stood there. 'You know what I'd like now?' Paul looked at her thoughtfully, clutching his stomach as he spoke. 'A nice warm bath. Tell that to your doctor friend. I didn't want a fix, I just wanted to get rid of the pain.'

'Maybe when you get home you can have one...'

Her words petered out and she kicked herself for her insensitivity as Paul gave a hollow laugh.

'There might be a bit of a line-up for the marble bathrooms at the viaduct. Don't worry about it.' Standing up, he gave a weary shrug. 'I'll be OK.'

'You can have a bath here.' The words tumbled out of her mouth without much thought, and even though Mary would be furious, even though Rory wanted him moved on, the patient was Eleanor's priority. 'I can see if we've got any clean clothes for you.'

'You'd do that?' He blinked at her. 'But what would your boss say?'

'Leave her to me.' Eleanor smiled. 'Wait there and I'll go and get the bathroom ready.'

Mary, as predicted, was furious. 'What on earth do you think you're doing, Eleanor? He'll have a bath and before you know it he'll be rolling on the floor screaming with pain and we'll be back to square one.'

'She's right,' Rory broke in. 'He's just playing for time.'

'He isn't,' Eleanor insisted. 'When I've got a stomachache, I want a bath, and I bet the two of you are the same.' She stared angrily at their guilty faces. 'So why should it be different for Paul?'

'Fine,' Mary bristled, 'he can have his bath.' As Rory went to speak, Mary spoke over him. 'You don't have to say it, Rory. *I'll* take him to his bath and help him in. Let's see how keen he is then.'

Maybe it wasn't such a bad thing she was leaving, Eleanor decided as Mary frogmarched Paul to the bathroom. If staying meant she was going to end up as cynical and as doubting as them, maybe she was better out of there.

Avoiding Rory, she hid in various cubicles every

time he wandered through, landing Pier with anything that might involve a conversation with the consultant.

'He's getting dressed,' Mary said an hour or so later. 'In the clothes you found for him.'

'Thank you,' Eleanor responded tartly, then smiled as Paul appeared in the corridor, a new man indeed with his hair washed and fresh clean clothes.

'You look great.' Eleanor smiled, making her way over. 'Did the bath help?'

'A lot.' Paul nodded. 'Look, thanks for this. You've been really nice.'

'No problem.'

'Eleanor, I couldn't have a couple of paracetamol, could I? The doctor said I could take them—it's just I haven't got any money.'

'No problem,' she said again, which it wasn't. It was just the bit where she had to ask Rory to write them up she wasn't much looking forward to.

'What does he want now?' Rory sighed as Eleanor retrieved the casualty card from the out-pile and handed it tentatively towards him. 'I told you he'd be after something.'

'Give him a break, Rory. He asked for two para-cetamol, it's hardly big league.' She looked over to where Paul stood patiently waiting. 'Come on, Rory, admit it. You've read him all wrong. Write these up and he'll be on his way.'

'Which you should be, too, Rory,' Mary said, tapping at her watch. 'It's after five. I thought you had to leave bang on time today.'

'I did,' Rory replied, scribbling the order on the card, 'but, as I said, I want to talk to Eleanor.'

There was nothing subtle about Eleanor's blush, and nothing subtle about the eyebrows that shot into

Mary's hairline. 'Well, I suppose she could have her meal break now, if that's all right with you, Eleanor.'

It wasn't all right. The last thing Eleanor wanted was another emotional confrontation with Rory, but with her two seniors staring at her she wasn't exactly in a position to refuse.

'Fine,' Eleanor said as casually as she could manage. 'I'll just get these paracetamol for Paul and I'll meet you in the coffee-room.'

Walking to the drug room, she tried to rehearse her speech, tried to fathom answers to the questions Rory would inevitably ask, work out how she could respond without telling him about the baby.

The baby.

Swiping her ID badge, her mind lingered on that thought. Now that she knew she was going home, had decided on a future, she was finally coming around to the idea that she was actually going to have a baby.

And they'd be OK.

Eleanor knew that in her heart.

At first she thought it was Mary, Rory even, as the door that was closing behind her was pushed open. Her smile as she turned around faded as she saw Paul standing before her. He kicked the door shut behind him, the expression on his face every bit the nasty piece Rory had called him.

'You shouldn't be in here, Paul.' Somehow she kept her voice even, offering him an out, trying to stay in control, to push aside the horror of her situation—shut in a drug room with an angry addict. 'Go and wait outside and I'll bring your paracetamol out to you.'

'I don't want paracetamol.' His voice was a menacing snarl, his hand gesturing to the door. 'Lock it,' he ordered.

'I don't want to do that.' Her voice was still calm. She looked him in the eye and tried to hide her fear. 'I want you to get out now, Paul.'

'Lock it.' His hand waved at her, a glint of metal catching the fluorescent light. If Eleanor had been scared before, she was terrified now, the sharp edge of a scalpel blade enough to render Paul's request delivered.

'Now,' he said as Eleanor's trembling hands snubbed the lock, 'open it.' He gestured furiously to the controlled drug cupboard. 'Open it,' he ordered again, impatience and agitation evident in his voice.

'I can't, Paul.' As his face contorted in fury she went on, 'It's locked. I haven't got the keys.'

'Bull!' His eyes were almost popping out of his head now. 'Use your card.' He pulled at the tag around her neck and the cord broke, just as Security had said it would if a patient ever grabbed it. She watched with mounting terror as he broached the cupboard, his fury escalating into a furious outburst when he saw the lock, realised Eleanor had been speaking the truth.

'I haven't got the keys, Paul,' Eleanor said again, frightened tears brimming in her eyes. She forced them back, desperately trying to stay calm, to form some plan, some way out of this horrible situation. 'Let me go, Paul. If you let me go now, with no harm done...'

'Shut up.' His eyes were glittering as he swung around.

'Paul, please,' Eleanor begged.

'Just shut up!' And whether it was his intention,

whether he meant to use it, he lunged forward and suddenly the scalpel was coming towards her. All she could think about was the baby she carried, maternal instinct crashing to the fore as she instinctively turned sideways, moved her stomach out of harm's way, her arms cradling her front as Paul fell against her.

'I didn't want to hurt you,' Paul was screaming as he righted himself and as Eleanor took a deep breath and turned her eyes towards him. 'I fell.'

'It's OK, Paul.' She went to straighten up, to somehow reason with him. 'I'm fine.'

She truly thought she was, but even before the words were out, she felt a sticky dampness on her blouse. She stared down at the spreading dark stain, her eyes widening in terror as realisation hit.

'I didn't mean it.' Still he ranted on and Eleanor just wanted him to be quiet, her hand pulling up at her blouse, craning her neck to see what he had inflicted, praying it was just a flesh wound. But as tiny stars started jumping in her eyes, as her hands moved to the bench to support herself, even in the absence of a decent view, Eleanor knew she had been stabbed.

'What have you done?' Staring aghast at her bloodied hand, the fear was now evident in her voice.

'You made me do it.' He was pacing now, agitated and furious, kicking at the walls as Eleanor sank back against the bench, sweat trickling between her breasts, the colour draining out of her face. But suddenly when all seemed lost hope flared.

'Eleanor.' Rory's voice was at the door, banging loudly on it. 'Eleanor, open up and let me in.'

'He can get the keys,' Paul snarled in a brutal whisper. 'You tell him to get back here with the keys. One false word and I swear I'll finish you off.'

Hauling her towards the door, he smacked her hand away as she went for the lock.

'Don't open it, just tell him to bring them.'

'It doesn't work like that,' Eleanor whispered urgently, shrinking back as he pushed a finger to her lips.

'Oh, yes, it does.'

'He'll know there's something wrong if I don't open the door.'

'An inch. And if your hero doctor pushes in, remember that there's a blade at the back of your neck.'

She had to get this right. Eleanor knew that, knew if there was any chance of getting out alive she had to convince Rory to do as she asked.

Rory would know, probably already knew, something terrible was happening, but with Paul in this agitated state it was imperative Rory just get the keys and hand them over.

She could feel the cool metal of the scalpel on the back of her neck as she fumbled with the door, feel the bile rising in her throat, her legs trembling violently as her blood pressure plummeted.

'Roy?' As he went to come in she shook her head. 'I'm busy in here. What do you need? I'll get it for you.'

There was the longest pause before he answered.

'I need you to come and set up that equipment, Eleanor. Now, please.' She could hear the tension behind his words, her deliberate mispronunciation of his name no doubt confirming his worst fears.

'OK.' As Paul pulled her hair down her back, Eleanor squeezed her eyes closed.

'I'll be there in a moment, but can you bring me the keys to the drug cupboard, *Roy?* I forgot them.'

Another long pause, and Eleanor held her breath as she awaited his response, praying he wouldn't blow things now, not sure he fully understood just how dire her situation was.

'Sure.' His voice was clipped, a muscle pounding in his cheek as he stared back at her, registering the utter fear in her eyes, the pale, terrified face. 'Do you remember what it was that I asked you to set up?'

'Of course.' Paul was pulling her hair harder now, letting her know none too gently it was time to wind things up. 'I really have to get on now.'

'But you always miss something.' Rory's voice was derisive. 'Every time I ask you to set up a trolley, you leave something out. Now, I want you to tell me again what it was I asked for.'

He was fishing now and Eleanor knew it, but it was imperative Paul didn't realise, imperative Paul didn't lose his cool again.

'You asked me for some O-neg blood,' Eleanor answered, telling him what he would need to treat her, eyes widening, tears brimming over as Rory's face seemed to dissolve before her eyes. 'An eighteen-gauge scalpel and…' Her voice trailed off. She'd told him what the weapon was, told him what was needed, but there was a piece of information she hadn't given him, one vital piece that was missing. And whatever her reasons for keeping things in, now wasn't the time for secrecy. If her baby was to stand a chance, quite simply Rory had to know.

'A BHCG test.' Her voice trembled as she said it, knowing how awful it must be for him to find out this way that she was pregnant. Knowing the agony she had just unleashed. But Paul was getting impatient now, yanking her head back further and pulling her inside as he simultaneously slammed the door.

'Arrogant shit!' he shouted as he released her. 'Talking to you like that. Will he bring them?' When Eleanor didn't answer he started shouting again. 'The keys, will he bring them?'

She nodded. That was all she had the strength to do. She sank to the floor, leaning against the bench, her head in her hands, and praying Rory would hurry, praying he wouldn't be long, wondering what was going on outside, the controlled panic that would be unleashed, the wheels that would click into motion as a code black was declared.

Oh, God, she hadn't thought of that. Panic kicked in as she realised the overhead chimes would go off soon, terrified of Paul's rage when he realised she had just shopped him.

Rory had thought about that, though. From the second he had hit the coffee-room, the second he had sat down and an awful sense of foreboding had crept through him, Rory had thought about nothing else.

Paul didn't want paracetamol.

Paul had never wanted paracetamol.

He wanted Eleanor in the drug room.

He had to be wrong. Please, God, let him be wrong. Running through the department, pounding on the locked door, he had waited, prayed for her beautiful, irritated face to frown at his intrusion as she opened the door. Instead, his worst fears had been confirmed.

That bastard had her in there.

His mind racing, adrenaline pumping through his veins, he ran the length of the unit, willing himself to stay calm, to focus, to do this right.

'The keys.' He was rummaging through Mary's

pockets as she jumped back, startled. 'Eleanor's locked in the drug room with Lang!'

'Eleanor.' Mary's wail of horror hadn't even ended before he barked his orders out. 'Set up Resus, get the surgeons down here. He's got a scalpel—I think he's used it on her.' He had the keys now and every fibre of him ached to go back to Eleanor, to get her the hell out of there, but he had to do this right, had to do everything he could to make her safe.

'Call a code black, but no loudspeaker. Make that very clear to Switchboard, and tell the police no sirens. I don't want anyone in that corridor.' He was turning to go now, but there was one more thing to be said, one more thing Mary really needed to know.

'I think she might be pregnant.'

CHAPTER TWELVE

NEVER had Eleanor felt more alone. Slumped against the bench, watching as her life force darkened her blouse, she could hear her breaths coming short and ragged, feel the flicker of the pulse in her neck as her heart fought to cope.

Why was Rory taking so long?

Time seemed to have taken on no meaning now, the eerie silence growing louder as she struggled to stay conscious. Paranoia crept in with every passing moment. Perhaps Rory hadn't understood the urgency in her eyes, had dismissed her rantings as if she were running true to form. Her mind was drifting now, off to her mother, her brothers, to the party she had missed for this awful night, and Eleanor chose to go there then, to focus on the image of a white marquee and a table heaving with food, to music that had filled her teens, to the joyous laughter that came when a family was united, to a safe place where the world was kind, utterly, blissfully oblivious to the chaos ripping through the hospital.

The fire doors slamming closed around the building as the wards shut down, smokers being dragged from the balconies and ordered into bed, visitors being urged back to their seats as head counts were taken, patients being swiftly wheeled out of Emergency as surgeons raced down. Ambulances, sirens wailing, then silenced as the vehicles swung into the driveway, turning around and heading elsewhere as Melbourne

Central was declared a no-go area, flashing their head-lights at the police cars that dashed towards the build-ing.

'Eleanor, I've got the keys you wanted.' She could hear Rory's sharp knock on the door, his voice con-fusingly normal, she could feel Paul's hand stinging her cheek over and over as he tried to pull her back to the world, tried to force her to stand, and she knew she should do it.

Should somehow find the strength to make it to the door, to get the keys from Rory and give Paul what he thought he needed, but all Eleanor longed to do was sleep.

To close her eyes and rest a while.

'Eleanor!' Rory's voice was more insistent now. 'I thought you said that you wanted the keys.'

'Get the keys from him,' Paul insisted, slapping her again. Forcing her eyes open, she stared back at her captor, but fear had left her now. Nothing more could hurt her. She heard the doorhandle, the sharp intake of breath as Paul realised his mistake, as he realised the door was unlocked, her lethargic, sunken eyes dragging to the door as Rory walked in.

'What the hell's going on?' She could hear him shouting, see his shocked expression as he pushed open the door and stepped inside, and so convincing was his act, in her hypoxic state even Eleanor won-dered if Rory hadn't realised what was taking place, if somehow he had missed the clues she had given him.

'Open the cupboard!' Grabbing her hair again, Paul seemingly remained in control, shouting his orders at a compliant Rory who headed straight for the cup-board, unlocking it in an instant then turning around.

'Take what you want.' Rory stood beside the open cupboard. 'Take what the hell you want and get the hell out of here. I need to get to her.'

'You really think I'm that stupid, don't you?' Paul was waving the scalpel now as he jerked her head back with the other hand, fear, anger in every movement, every word. 'If I take one step out of this room the cops will be on me.'

'They won't.' Rory shook his head fiercely. 'They don't even know that you're here.'

'You expect me to believe that?'

You have to do this right.

The words pounded over and over in Rory's head, his training coming to the fore when it was really needed, a hostage negotiation article that had pinged into his inbox and made interesting reading over a morning coffee all amalgamating now, telling him that how he dealt with this, how he played these next few moments could be life or death for Eleanor.

And his child.

Forcibly he snapped that out of his mind, pushed it away with all the mental force he could muster. Emotions had to take a back seat now.

Wrenching his eyes from Eleanor, he focused on her captor.

Get him on side.

Make him think he's winning.

'How did you get in here, Paul?' His question was pure indignation, as if Paul had somehow wandered in uninvited to an invitation-only party, as if Eleanor wasn't lying bleeding on the floor. 'Come on, I need to know how long you've been in here. I was just talking to Eleanor, I told her—'

'To lay up a trolley,' Paul snarled, his lips sneering

in a superior grin. 'Yeah, I heard you. I heard you talking to her like she was a piece of dirt on your shoe. She was the only one who was nice to me.' Hysteria was creeping into his voice. 'She was nice to me.' Letting go of her hair, he waved one hand while the scalpel hovered dangerously at her throat.

Rory broke in quickly. The situation was accelerating way out of control, the mental move he had planned as he'd run towards the drug room taking on dire proportions now. 'Eleanor told me to bring the keys. She told me that she needed them. That's why I'm here, Paul. When am I supposed to have had a chance to call the police?' He stared at the pathetic attempt of a man and tried to keep the contempt from his eyes. 'Are you telling me that you were in here all along? That you were actually here when I came to the door?'

Slowly Paul nodded, a malicious grin spreading over his face as Rory stood stock still, every muscle taut, his pulse pounding in his ears, desperate to get to where Eleanor lay, for this nightmare to be over. Her colour was ashen now, eyes that had stared at him as he entered unseeing now, that gorgeous shock of hair dark with sweat, her breathing rapid and shallow. Rory decided there and then that if his hastily formed plan didn't work, if Paul didn't believe he had walked in unawares, then he would have to tackle him. His mind was working overtime now, desperate plans forming as he planned his next move. He didn't care about Paul, didn't care about his own safety, it didn't even enter the equation. But two men fighting in this confined space as she lay there helpless, that scalpel so close to her throat, made it an unappealing option. But if this didn't work, it was the only one he had.

'Fill a bag.'

Make him think he's winning.

Deliberately Rory held in check the relief that flooded him, scooping out the contents of the cupboard with one hand, tossing the bag at Paul and hoping, praying that was it.

'There's no police?' Paul checked. His hand was on the door now, Eleanor forgotten in the haste to get his fix, and it would have been so easy for Rory to lunge at him, to use the tackles he'd learnt playing rugby and floor him in one move, but all he could think of was Eleanor. All he wanted was this man out of the way. What happened to him after that didn't even merit a thought.

'Just take them,' Rory roared, as Paul finally wrenched open the door and fled.

In one movement Rory was over Eleanor, scooping her up in his arms and lunging for the door. Eleanor wanted to tell him it was OK, wanted to tell him to slow down, but it was as if she were watching things from afar, like falling asleep on the sofa with the television on, aware what was going on but unable to respond.

'Help me!' She heard his shout, could hear his steps running across the polished floor, vaguely registering how strange it was that there were no patients, utterly oblivious to the fact that for the first time in the thirty years it had stood, the emergency department at Melbourne Central had only one patient.

She could hear the Resus doors sliding open, lay on the bed with staring eyes as surgeons slapped her hands to find a vein.

'You're going to be OK, pet.' Mary's voice was soothingly familiar, gentle hands working her brow as scissors razored through her clothes, a sting of shame as she lay naked and exposed, but Mary sensed it instantly and covered her.

'Chest X-ray,' the surgeon was shouting. 'The scalpel could have pierced her lung.'

'She might be pregnant!' Rory's voice was a primal roar, and the surgeon's came back icily calm.

'The patient's my priority.' He seemed to relent, maybe saw the anguish in her eyes over the green oxygen mask. 'Put a catheter in and get a urine test.'

'We don't need a urine test.' Mary's was the voice of reason, sensible old-school hands prodding Eleanor's abdomen. 'Her fundus is over the pelvic brim.' She flicked back the blanket, glancing at the swollen breasts, then replaced it, her voice firm and clear as she addressed the surgeon. 'The patient is pregnant, Doctor.'

'I want her in Theatre.' The surgeon's request was unequivocal. 'I'll go ahead and scrub. Get a catheter in then push the blood through as you run her up there.'

'You'll be all right, pet.' Mary's face was back in focus now, that beautiful Irish face lined with concern, but as much as Eleanor loved her, as much as she wanted Mary there, it was Rory she needed, Rory. Her eyes raked the room to find him as the blood seeping into her veins finally rallied her a notch.

'Rory?'

'He's outside.' Mary's voice was unwavering. 'He's just making sure that everything goes smoothly, that Theatre's ready for you. Now, you just rest, pet, concentrate on getting well.'

'I don't want to die.' It was the first time she'd acknowledged it, really acknowledged the direness of her situation, and as terror started to mount, as fear gripped her by the throat, Mary's eyes held hers.

'You're not going to die, Eleanor,' Mary said firmly. 'Not on my shift.'

CHAPTER THIRTEEN

'YOU'RE supposed to be out with Gary?' Eleanor's voice was a mere croak and she struggled to pull the oxygen mask off as Pier's tearful face came into focus.

'What? And miss the drama?' Pier rolled red-rimmed eyes. 'You know how I love men in uniform.'

He started blowing his nose and in her drug-induced state Eleanor wondered if he had a cold, wondered if perhaps the pollen count was exceptionally high, because Mary was standing over her now, also with red-rimmed eyes and a tissue in her hand.

'I'm sorry.' Eleanor was crying now. It was all coming back as she rolled her head on the pillow, the horrors of what had taken place starting to trickle in, her eyes screwing closed as she attempted to block out the images. 'You told me to look both ways before I went in the drug room, warned me—'

'Hush now,' Mary soothed, as a nurse pressed a button, inflating the blood-pressure cuff strapped to her arm, changing the oxygen mask over to nasal prongs as Mary chatted away. 'You know me—I can talk under water. Sure, if I wanted to I could give you a lecture about the pillow you're lying on, tell you that in old days the opening faced away from the door...' Her voice trailed off, her hands squeezing Eleanor's tighter. 'You're safe now, pet, that's all that matters.'

'Rory?' As soon as the word was out she regretted

it, shrinking back on the pillow, chiding herself for indiscretion. 'He didn't get hurt? Paul didn't attack him?'

'Mr Lang,' Mary said tightly, 'is safely behind bars where he deserves to be. And, no, Eleanor, he didn't hurt Rory. He took the drugs and ran straight into the arms of the police. But don't think about that now, my girl. Right now all you have to do is concentrate on getting better.'

Eleanor nodded glumly, closing her eyes as Pier fiddled wih the fit of her nasal prongs, slipping back to an unwelcome sleep, but with too many questions still buzzing in her head, her eyes snapped open and met Mary's.

'I need to talk to Rory.'

'He's on the phone, pet.' Mary's hand was stroking her brow again. 'Trying to get hold of your mum. She should be back from the party soon. You need to rest…'

But she couldn't rest, couldn't just lie there with so much unsaid, couldn't just cling to the hand that was holding hers when, however well meant, however comforting, it was quite simply the wrong one. She needed to see Rory. It was the only thought in her mind. She needed to see Rory, needed to tell him properly about the baby…

'Mary!' A whimper escaped her lips, her hand struggling for freedom as she moved them in an instinctive movement to her stomach, the baby pinging into her consciousness, answers desperately needed now.

'Lie back, pet,' Mary soothed. 'Lie back and rest…'

'But the baby…' Mary's mouth was moving but

Eleanor couldn't hear a word as Rory's grey face came into focus. He looked older and more tired than she had ever seen him, the suit discarded, now in theatre blues, a shadow dusting his chin as eyes filled with tears met hers.

'Can you leave us, please?' His voice was the most welcome sound she had ever heard, those eyes that stared down at hers all she needed now as Mary, clucking like a broody hen, tucked the blanket a little tighter and shot Rory a menacing look. It took a lot of sweet talking from Pier before he finally managed to prise her away.

'The baby?' There was so much more she needed to know, so much more that needed to be said, but for now, at least, only one thing mattered.

'The baby's still there,' Rory said gently, but he swallowed hard for a moment, perching himself on the bed, dragging a deep breath into his lungs. 'The scalpel lacerated your kidney, Eleanor, you lost an awful lot of blood. Mr Kemp managed to repair it, you've still got both kidneys...'

'I don't think he meant to stab me.' As Rory exhaled loudly, his fists clenched into tight balls, Eleanor tried to carry on talking, but Rory overrode her.

'He had a scalpel, Eleanor, he locked you in a drug room with him, for God's sake. Not even you can turn this around.'

'I'm not trying to,' she whispered, her eyes imploring him to understand, to listen to her take on this. 'But he was desperate, Rory. I don't think it was ever his intention to use it.'

'He nearly killed you, Eleanor. You could still...' His mouth closed firmly, his lips in a thin taut line, and Eleanor knew he was holding back, knew he hadn't quite finished, knew from the tone of his voice that her torture wasn't quite over.

'Miscarry?'

He was holding her hand now, but she pulled it away as he nodded grimly. She didn't want his sympathy, crocodile tears for a baby he surely couldn't want.

'You lost a lot of blood,' he said again, the muscles on his jaw quilting as he tried to keep his voice even. 'Mr Kemp had a hell of a job to save your kidney. It was a long operation and sometimes…'

'I could still lose the baby?'

Rory nodded slowly. 'We'll just have to take things a day at a time.'

We. The single word resonated in her mind, taunting her, ramming home all that could never be.

Turning her head away from him, she stared unseeingly at the monitors that surrounded her.

'I won't tell anyone it's yours. No one needs to know.'

'Eleanor.' His voice was urging her to face him but still she looked away. 'Of course they're going to know…'

Finally she turned, her blue eyes looking up at him. 'Not from me, they're not. Why do you think I'm leaving, Rory? I never intended them to find out, I never wanted to embarrass you.'

'Embarrass me?' He shook his head, bewildered, raking a hand through his hair as he struggled to stay calm, to hold in the angry, raw questions he wanted to hurl at her, knowing now simply wasn't the time.

'I embarrass you, don't I? That's why you didn't ask me out that night in the ambulance bay.' Restraint was the last thing on her mind, tortured, half-cooked thoughts coming to the fore. 'You didn't want me to embarrass you at your sister's fortieth.'

'Never say that, Eleanor. You could never embarrass me. I was embarrassed for myself.'

'But why?'

'Because you're right. I *was* going to ask you to come that night. If you hadn't said what you did, I would have.' He watched her frown, watched the endearing way she nibbled on her lip as she struggled to remember the conversation. And even if it was for the last time, even if she was going to snatch her hand away again, he didn't hold back. As his hand reached for hers he let it follow its natural course, held those slender fingers in his palm, eternally grateful when she let them rest there. 'You've got a short-term memory problem, you know?' He sniffed, not very gracious perhaps, but tears were coming and he simply couldn't bear to let her go.

'Only when you're around,' Eleanor admitted. 'What did I say to make you change your mind? What did I say that stopped you asking me along?'

'There you were, talking about twenty-first birthdays when I've been to maybe five fortieth birthdays this year. We're at different stages, Eleanor, looking for different things…'

'Bruce, Gina's brother, turns forty next year.' Her eyes were closing, her answer delivered, as if it were all that simple, as if it were all that easy.

As if age didn't matter a jot, as if the raised eyebrow and winks from his family wouldn't have affected her. And maybe they wouldn't have. Who knew? Even the guffaws from his rugby mates at his spectacular choice in women might have raised no more than a smile from her—those frail shoulders were obviously stronger than they looked.

'Why didn't you tell me about the baby?' he asked, because quite simply he had to. Couldn't let her close her eyes again, without at least knowing that. 'Were you going to leave without me even knowing?'

Her eyes stayed closed but her tiny nod tore through him.

'Were you going to have…?' His voice trailed off, his jaw clenching as he struggled to stay calm, struggled to understand the woman he had thought he knew.

'No,' she answered his unfinished question, tears streaming her eyes as she finally managed to look at him. 'I wasn't going to have an abortion. I was going to go back to the country and try to pick up the pieces of my life, try to make something of the mess I'd made for myself.'

'What ever did you say to her?' Mary was back, digging out a tissue from her sleeve and wiping the never-ending tears. 'I got through to your mum, pet. She's on her way as we speak. She'll be here before the morning.'

'Is she OK?' Eleanor's heart went out to her mother, imagining her picking up the phone, hearing the awful news and breaking it to her father. 'She'll be so worried.'

'That's what mums do best.' Mary smiled. 'But I told her you were going to be fine and…' she shot a defiant look at Rory '…I told her I wasn't going to leave your side till she got here.'

It was easier to sleep, easier to close her eyes as the two of them bickered, listen to the blips of the monitor as it ticked away, the hiss of the blood-pressure cuff every fifteen minutes as it relayed her obs, the alarm on the IVAC pump as her final unit of blood was delivered. Opening her eyes, she stared up at a nurse, who actually looked younger than her, changing the empty flask over to saline, punching in the drip rate before smiling at her.

'You look a lot better.'

Eleanor gave a small nod, struggling to sit up, but the nurse pushed her gently back down. 'Your blood pressure's still a bit on the low side. Just lie there a while.'

'Where are they?' Casting her eye over the empty chairs, Eleanor frowned. 'Did they go home?'

'They were told to take their "discussion" into the waiting room by the nurse supervisor no less, can you imagine? The senior emergency nurse and the consultant behaving like a couple of rowdy teenagers.' She gave a tiny almost imperceptible wink. 'Don't tell them I told you.'

'I won't.'

'You gave us all a fright,' the nurse went on. 'Half the hospital must have stayed back till you came out of Theatre and Mr Kemp said that you were going to be OK. The canteen even stayed open.'

'But why?' Eleanor shook her head, bewildered. 'I've only been here a few months, I hardly know anyone.'

'You're one of us,' the nurse said simply, her pretty face snapping into a frown as Rory tentatively approached.

'Ten minutes,' she warned sternly. 'And then she's to rest. Her parents are only half an hour away. I don't want any repeats from before.'

'There won't be.' For a brute of a male he looked

positively sheepish, and Eleanor bit back a faint smile as he gingerly sat down.

'And to think I was worried about facing your father.' He rolled his eyes. 'You should have heard Mary. The obstetrician came down,' he explained. 'Up to that point Mary had assumed you were pregnant by someone from back home. They're pretty accurate, the scans at this stage. They can pinpoint the age to almost the day of…' His voice trailed off. 'She thought you just had a crush on me, that's why she's been guarding you like a broody hen tonight. She'd even decided that that might be why you'd chosen to leave Melbourne and she was worried I'd put my great big feet in it and upset you further. But when she realised we had actually….' Eleanor would have blushed, but with a haemoglobin of eight, instead she acknowledged his, staring back sadly at the man she simply couldn't have.

'I've got a duty of care, Eleanor,' he explained gently. 'Not just to my patients, but also to the staff under me. Consultants aren't supposed to have flings with pretty young nurses. It happens, I know, but when it does, when inevitably it ends…' He gave a small, tense shrug. 'The nurse ends up leaving. I've seen it over and over, but never, not for a moment did I think it would happen to me.'

'Well, it did,' Eleanor said flatly. 'And your prediction was spot on, given that I'm leaving.'

'I ended it so you wouldn't have to,' Rory said firmly. 'Ended it, thinking no one would find out, that you'd be able to fulfill your dreams, have the career you wanted…'

'I wanted you!' She didn't want to cry again, didn't want to embarrass herself any more than she had already, so she bit the tears back, swallowing them down as she screwed her eyes closed. 'When we made love that night I thought it was a beginning, thought it was the start of something really special, and you were already imagining the end. Why?' Pleading eyes opened. 'Why were you so sure it was going to end?'

'Because it would have,' Rory insisted. 'Eleanor, I didn't want a fling, didn't want a hole-in-the-corner affair. I think I fell in love with you before I even properly saw you.' He registered her frown and despite the pain, despite the agony of the night, a smile twitched on his lips as he recalled their first meeting.

'Loved me?' Whatever they were giving her through the drip, it was working. Sure she must have misheard, misunderstood, she closed her eyes, shook her head, waited for the mist to clear. But when she opened them again, he was still staring, still there.

'A bossy little nurse who, no matter how she tried, no matter how fierce she acted, simply couldn't stop herself from being nice. Couldn't stop herself apologising for shaving my leg or taking my last ten dollars. I wanted a bit of anonymity,' Rory said, 'an agency nurse I would never have to face again. Instead, I hobbled away wondering what you looked like, if I'd ever get a chance to see you again.'

His hand gripped hers then and this time she didn't pull it away, just let him hold it, the quiet strength of his touch somehow imbuing her. 'I fell in love with you all over again when we rowed about the morphine. I've been crazy about you from the day you burst into my life, wanting to get to know you better, wanting to take you out...'

'Then why didn't you? Why did you sleep with me, only to regret it the next day?'

'I didn't regret it.' His words confused her. 'I could never regret it. It was the most special night of my life, Eleanor. But it shouldn't have happened, should never have happened...'

'Why?'

He gave a low laugh, shaking his head in disbelief at her utter failure to see his point. 'I'm thirty-five years old, Eleanor. And though I never have before, the second I held you, loved you, all of a sudden I was a thirty-five-year-old guy who's thinking about babies and marriage and all the things you said at the outset you didn't want.'

'I didn't,' Eleanor said indignantly, but her mouth snapped closed as Rory nodded firmly.

'Oh, yes, you did, Eleanor. You told me that the last thing on earth you wanted was marriage and a baby.'

'Oh.'

'That all you wanted to do was concentrate on your career.'

'Oh.'

'Is everything all right?' The nurse was back, smiling at Eleanor and frowning at Rory at the same time, prompting Eleanor to push her pain-control button, listening to the ping and whir of her PCA machine as the medication was delivered.

'Fine.' Eleanor nodded, her mind struggling with a blood pressure below a hundred and a rather hefty dose of pethidine, trying to somehow work a way out of yet another corner she'd backed herself into.

'She looks too young to be a nurse,' Eleanor said vaguely, as the nurse drifted away.

'Maybe you're just getting older.' He smiled but his heart wasn't in it. He watched that proud, wary face, struggling to focus, those beautiful red lips, way too pale, trying and failing not to picture her on an operating table. He felt sick, not just because it had happened, but because it had happened to Eleanor.

To the youngest, sweetest, most trusting of them all.

'I don't want marriage or babies.' Her pupils were practically pinpoint from the drugs, the china blue of her eyes glittering as she attempted to focus, her words slurring as if she'd drunk a bottle of champagne. And he wished so much that she had, that he'd at least done that for her, taken her out and really spoiled her, just once even. Wished they were lying on her new sofa with two empty glasses and a whole night of wonder ahead of them.

She didn't deserve this.

'Don't worry about it now,' Rory said sadly. 'Just rest, Eleanor.'

'I mean, I don't want to be a mum…'

'We'll sort something out.' His hand still held hers, trying to be strong as each word just lacerated him further. 'When you're feeling better, when you're stronger, we'll sort something out. Whatever you decide to do, I'll support you in any way I can. But right now all you really need to do is have a sleep.'

'I don't want to sleep.' She was getting restless now, pulling at the nasal prongs, struggling to sit up. Rory pushed the call bell for the nurse, alarm growing as the cuff on the blood-pressure machine inflated again, nurses appearing from everywhere as Rory called for assistance.

'Increasing agitation.' He was barking out orders now. 'Pulse rate's up. What's her obs doing?'

'Rory.' All eyes turned to her, her voice bristling with indignation as a cast of thousands gathered around, the pethidine taking away her last ounce of self-restraint. 'I'm not about to collapse again. I'm just trying to tell you that I love you.

'Love you,' she repeated, as the staff melted away and the only person that mattered in all this remained. 'I'm not on the lookout for a husband, I don't have a burning desire to be a mum.' Her free hand fluttered down to her stomach, holding the life within as Rory's hand cupped hers, willing their little one just to hang in there. 'But I want *this* baby, Rory. Do you understand that?' He did, nodding his understanding, tears filling his eyes as she bravely carried on. 'And I want you, too. Not a consultant, not a potential husband. I just want you, Rory.'

'You've got me,' he rasped, his voice thick with emotion. 'You always have had, Eleanor.'

She could feel the warmth of his hand on her stomach spreading through her, stirring what looked like the first rays of hope into shape.

'It will be fine,' Rory said firmly, definitely. 'Our baby is going to be fine.'

'Your parents are here.' Mary's flushed face appeared at the bedside. 'They're talking to Mr Kemp and then they'll be in.'

'Oh, poor Mum,' Eleanor moaned. 'She must be exhausted.'

'Don't worry about it,' Rory soothed. 'She'll be OK. Once she's seen you, once her mind's been put at ease, I'll take her over to your flat and she can have a rest. Things will all seem better in the morning…'

An appalling thought suddenly sprang to mind and it had nothing to do with her mother's reaction to the bombsite of a flat she'd left this morning and everything to do with Rory's.

'You can't.' Worried eyes met his. 'You can't possibly take her over there.'

'Why?' The first real smile of the night twitched on his lips. 'What with you being so compulsively tidy, I'll bet the place is spotless, and if there's nothing to eat we can always crack open the olives.'

'You knew,' Eleanor mumbled, sinking down under the sheet a touch.

'I'm sure the furthest thing from your mother's mind is a bit of mess,' Mary broke in, completely missing the point. 'Now, Eleanor.' Given the maternal gushings of before, Mary's voice was positively stern now. 'Did you, or did you not, tell you parents that I said that unless you worked tonight you'd lose your job?'

'Maybe…' Eleanor mumbled, the pethidine not quite strong enough to take away her sting of shame.

'So it's all your fault.' Rory managed a half-smile, looking across at his colleague for a brief moment before turning his attention back to Eleanor.

'I wouldn't be feeling so sure of yourself, young man. You haven't seen the size of Eleanor's father. And how many brothers is it you've got, pet?'

'Three.'

He was gazing at her now, the sight of the drips, the machines fading as those blue eyes held his, the trust and love that blazed there all he needed to make things right.

'Would it soften the blow if I told them,' Rory started, his Adam's apple bobbing up and down as he tentatively continued, 'that the reason you were working tonight was to get the whole of next week off?'

'Perhaps.' Eleanor nodded, knowing what was coming, her lips quivering in anticipation as Rory slowly, softly stroked her cheek.

'That we were going to drive to your parents' tomorrow so I could ask your father for your hand in marriage?' She couldn't answer, the words strangling in her throat as dreams she hadn't even known existed suddenly all came true. 'Do you think that might help when we tell them about our baby?'

'Yes.' It was all she could manage, but it was the only word Rory needed to hear. His lips found hers, kissing her softly, gently but with so much love Eleanor never wanted it to end.

'Here.' Mary was pulling her own engagement ring off and handing it to Rory.

'They'll spot the difference when I buy Eleanor one,' Rory protested.

'Do they not teach doctors anything in medical school?' Mary tutted, pushing on the ring and wrapping a wad of tape around it. 'It would have been taped up when they rushed her to Theatre. I'll go and stall them.'

'I love you,' Eleanor whispered, when finally they were alone.

'I love you, too,' Rory replied, simply, honestly, but a tiny frown remained.

'And before you say it, you're not.'

'Not what?' he asked, his frown deepening.

'Too old for me.'

'I never said I was.'

'You were about to.' She smiled back at him, the love she saw blazing in his eyes giving her all the confidence she needed to finally say exactly what was in her heart. 'I win all around, Rory. I've got twelve years on you.'

'It's the other way around,' Rory whispered, but she shook her head against the pillow, the pethidine really kicking in now, pushing her down into the sweetest sleep that she'd had for a long, long time, her eyes regretfully shutting on his beautiful face. 'I've got twelve more years than you had of waking up beside someone I love,' she mumbled as he gazed down at her. 'Twelve more years of being loved and cherished.'

'You will be,' Rory promised, as finally her mind switched off, the bliss of sleep washing over her.

Bending down, he kissed her pale cheek again. 'You will be.'

EPILOGUE

'THANK you so much for this.' Mary smiled brightly as Eleanor tentatively made her way over to the whiteboard. 'I was tearing my hair out, couldn't get an agency nurse, and then Rory suggested I try you. He said that your mum was down for the week, looking after Matilda. How's my favourite god-daughter doing?'

'She's great,' Eleanor gulped, wondering why on earth she'd agreed to this. For a few weeks now Rory had been hinting that she do the odd shift, that maybe she'd enjoy getting back to nursing. And so far she'd managed to put it off, saying that Matilda was too young to be left, that she was still breastfeeding, that working together mightn't be such a good idea, tossing up reasons why she couldn't go back. But Mary's call had come out of the blue. Desperate for staff she had begged her to come in, catching Eleanor completely unawares, until, against her better judgement, she'd agreed to come in for a shift. 'It doesn't look very busy.' Eleanor eyed the department suspiciously, 'I thought you said the place was full, fit to burst.'

'It was when I rang you.' Mary shrugged. 'But you know what this place is like—full one minute, empty the next.'

'Hi, there.' Rory came over, smiling down at her. 'How are you feeling?'

'Nervous,' Eleanor admitted, staring around the department she hadn't seen for a year now, fiddling with

180

the name band around her neck and waiting for the
horrors of her last shift to overwhelm her.

They didn't.

Her eyes worked the department, peering into the
Resus room, glimpsing the equipment that lined the
walls, but it was a nervous excitement that was filling
her now, a need to get back in there, to get on with
the job she'd been born to do.

But she wasn't about to tell Rory that!

'You've nothing to be nervous about,' Rory insisted. 'Everything's the same as when you left it—
except for the drug cupboard, of course.'

'The old way's the best way,' Mary butted in, and
Rory rolled his eyes. 'All the drugs are in the central
area now, where they used to be, and a security guard
is permanently on duty in the emergency department.'

'Can I talk to my wife, please, Mary,' Rory said
pointedly, 'without you putting your ten cents' worth
in?'

But Mary just shrugged at his irritated tone. 'She
might be your wife at home, Rory, but as I told you
before, she's a member of my nursing staff when
she's here.'

'*She's* also capable of speaking for herself,'
Eleanor retorted, swinging her eyes from one to the
other. 'Can I have a word with you in private, please,
Mr Hunter?'

'How's Matilda?' Rory pulled her aside, one hand
gently holding her elbow.

'Don't try and butter me up that way,' Eleanor
grumbled, then relented momentarily. 'Gorgeous. I've
fed her and Mum's going to take her for a walk then
put her down for her sleep. Mum said that she'd bring

her over in the pram when she's due for her evening feed, and I'll take my meal break then.

'Rory?' A frown puckered her brow, accusing eyes staring up at his. 'This was all a set-up, wasn't it? There's hardly a patient in the department and there's more staff on than I can count. You cooked this up with Mary to get me to come back, didn't you?'

'And your mum.' Rory grinned, not looking remotely sheepish. 'It was her idea, actually. Eleanor, you haven't set foot in the place since...' He didn't say it, they both knew what he was referring to. 'And it made sense for a while. You were too sick at first and what with the scare we had I understood when you didn't want to work while you were pregnant. But don't let Paul Lang win, Eleanor, don't let him change who you are.'

'He hasn't,' Eleanor said through gritted teeth. 'It's my priorities that have changed, not me.'

'I know.' Rory shrugged. 'You may be a wife and mother now, but you're still the sexiest, funniest, most independent woman I know.'

'People might talk...'

'Why? You're a consultant's wife.' Rory grinned. 'You're a respectable woman now.'

'And Matilda's only four months old,' Eleanor retorted. 'I should be at home with her.'

'And you will be,' Rory replied easily. 'Tonight, when your shift is over, we'll go home together.' He gave a small wink. 'We could pick up some noodles on the way.'

'You had no right,' Eleanor insisted. 'It's not as if I need to work.'

'Oh, yes, you do,' Rory said slowly. 'You're

twenty-four years old, Eleanor. Being an emergency nurse was your dream—'

'It still is,' she broke in, but her voice wavered. 'But I'm a mum now.'

'So is Karen, so is Caitlin and in a few weeks Vicki will be, too. You need other people around you, need to use that brain of yours. You miss it, I know you do. You're bored just being at home and you know it.'

He was right, well, sort of. She wasn't bored exactly. She adored Matilda, adored being a mum, but sometimes… Her eyes lingered around the department she loved, a department that, even though she had been away, she had never really left, Rory regaling her night after night with the endless tales the emergency department provided, popping down to the pub on the occasional Friday evening to share a drink and a chat with the staff who would always be friends.

'You belong here as much as I do, Eleanor.' He gave a soft smile before he pulled his hand away, snapping back into consultant mode, determined, hard as it would be, not to give her favours. 'Can you do a set of obs for me in cubicle four?'

She hesitated, but only for a second, heading to the nurses' station and rummaging in the drawer for a stethoscope.

It was right that she was here.

And as much as she'd never give him the satisfaction of knowing, Eleanor silently acknowledged that Rory had been right to force her back, to push her to be all she could be.

A wife, a mother, a nurse, a friend.

With Rory beside her she could have it all.

'Forget it!' A very pretty agency nurse rolled her

eyes as Eleanor walked past on her way to cubicle two. 'I've been trying to chat Rory Hunter up all morning and I didn't so much as get a smile out of him. I reckon he must be gay or something.'

Eleanor just shrugged, picking up the casualty card from outside cubicle four as the agency nurse still hovered. 'I'm Ann Marie, by the way, Ann Marie Jenkins. What's your name?'

'Eleanor.' Eleanor smiled very sweetly, taking quiet satisfaction as the young nurse's cheeks suitably darkened. 'Mrs Eleanor Hunter.'

Christmas is a time for miracles...

Christmas
Deliveries

Caroline Anderson   Marion Lennox

Sarah Morgan

On sale 3rd December 2004

*Available at most branches of WHSmith, Tesco, ASDA, Martins,
Borders, Eason, Sainsbury's and all good paperback bookshops.*

WE VALUE YOUR OPINION!

YOUR CHANCE TO WIN A ONE YEAR SUPPLY OF YOUR FAVOURITE BOOKS.

If you are a regular UK reader of Mills & Boon® Medical Romance™ and have always wanted to share your thoughts on the books you read—here's your chance:

Join the Reader Panel today!

This is your opportunity to let us know exactly what you think of the books you love.

And there's another great reason to join:

Each month, all members of the Reader Panel have a chance of winning four of their favourite Mills & Boon romance books EVERY month for a whole year!

If you would like to be considered for the Reader Panel, please complete and return the following application. Unfortunately, as we have limited spaces, we cannot guarantee that everyone will be selected.

Name: _____

Address: _____

_____ Post Code: _____

Home Telephone: _____ Email Address: _____

Where do you normally get your Mills & Boon Medical Romance books (please tick one of the following)?

Shops ❑   Library/Borrowed ❑

Reader Service™ ❑ If so, please give us your subscription no. _____

Please indicate which age group you are in:

16 – 24 ❑   25 – 34 ❑

35 – 49 ❑   50 – 64 ❑   65 + ❑

If you would like to apply by telephone, please call our friendly Customer Relations line on **020 8288 2886**, or get in touch by email to readerpanel@hmb.co.uk

Don't delay, apply to join the Reader Panel today and help ensure the range and quality of the books you enjoy.

Send your application to:

The Reader Service, Reader Panel Questionnaire, FREEPOST NAT1098, Richmond, TW9 1BR

If you do not wish to receive any additional marketing material from us, please contact the Data Manager at the address above.

MILLS & BOON

**Volume 6
on sale from
3rd December
2004**

Lynne
Graham

International Playboys

*The Winter
Bride*

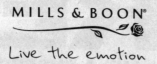

FREE

4 BOOKS AND A SURPRISE GIFT!

We would like to take this opportunity to thank you for reading this
Mills & Boon® book by offering you the chance to take FOUR more
specially selected titles from the Medical Romance™ series absolutely
FREE! We're also making this offer to introduce you to the benefits of
the Reader Service™—

- ★ **FREE home delivery**
- ★ **FREE gifts and competitions**
- ★ **FREE monthly Newsletter**
- ★ **Books available before they're in the shops**
- ★ **Exclusive Reader Service offers**

Accepting these FREE books and gift places you under no obligation
to buy; you may cancel at any time, even after receiving your free
shipment. Simply complete your details below and return the entire
page to the address below. You don't even need a stamp!

YES! Please send me 4 free Medical Romance books and a surprise
gift. I understand that unless you hear from me, I will receive 6
superb new titles every month for just £2.69 each, postage and packing
free. I am under no obligation to purchase any books and may cancel
my subscription at any time. The free books and gift will be mine to
keep in any case.   M4ZEE

Ms/Mrs/Miss/Mr.................................Initials ....
                                                              BLOCK CAPITALS PLEASE

Surname ....

Address ....

....

....Postcode ....

Send this whole page to:
The Reader Service, FREEPOST CN81, Croydon, CR9 3WZ